3-9-23

The Bones of Kekionga

The Bones of Kekionga

Jim Pickett

First Edition – 2017

First Editor Copyright – 2017
by Jim Pickett

ISBN: 978-0-9907862-6-9
3 4 5 6 7 8 9 10

OAK CREEK
media
Bluffton, Indiana

Dedication

This book is dedicated to those who came before us and to the generations yet to come, so they can remember our past.

Acknowledgement

A special thanks goes out to the Allen County Public Library of Fort Wayne, Indiana; The Genealogy Department of the Allen County Public Library, Fort Wayne, Indiana; The Lincoln Financial Foundation Collection at Allen County Public Library, Fort Wayne, Indiana; The History Center, Fort Wayne, Indiana; Kentucky Gateway Museum Center, Maysville, Kentucky; Ed Schwartz, Bluffton, Indiana; Jacob Pickett of Fort Wayne and to the many relatives and friends who have been beneficial and supportive in this project.

Introduction

The 1790 Battle of Kekionga, also known as Harmar's Defeat, was the culmination of frustrating attempts by American settlers and Native Americans to live peaceably among one another. Even though there were differing accounts leading up to, during and after this battle, over sixty sources were researched in an effort to maintain accuracy.

The author interwove what may have happened from both the Native American and American viewpoints. Although some activities are at the liberty of the writer, eighty per cent of the names in this historical fiction account were actual people. Prepare yourself to go back in time to 1912 and then to 1790.

Photo – Jim Pickett

Fort Wayne, Indiana - 1790

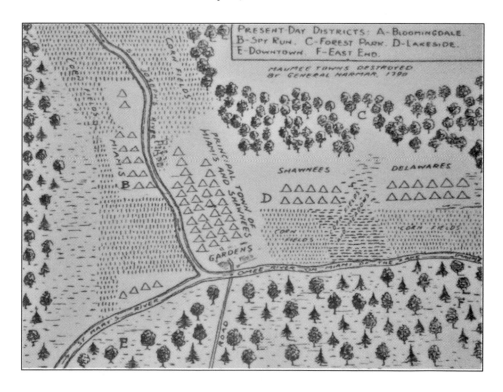

From <u>The Military Journal of Major Ebenezer Denny</u>
Officer in the Revolutionary and Indian War

Chapter One

"Hey, Nyle, dang it! I hit somethin' here just like that last house! I'm tellin' ya, this time we gotta tell the authorities."

"Let's dig down a little more, Stan, just to make sure. I'll help ya."

As the construction-working brothers plant a spade and cast a pick into the footer trench of a new house, more objects are struck, jarring the shovel handle of Stan's hand.

"Dag nabit, who do we contact?" says Stan as he now clears away the dirt and debris with his hands. "No way these are rocks. Look at this! These are bones, but danggg. Check out the cut marks and gashes. Nyle, somethin' bad happened here."

"Yeah, I see it," his coworker replies. "That last house we put the foundation in at had damaged bones, too."

"Oh my gosh," Stan gasps, as he breaks up some more soil, "This looks like a, a skull!"

"Ya found something, didn't ya?" declares a loud voice from the St Joseph River bank 100 feet away overlooking the construction site. The two workers momentarily stare at each other stunned, then look in the direction of the voice.

"I've been watching you guys workin' for a few minutes," the stranger exclaims, waiting for a trolley to pass by on St. Joe Boulevard. Limping across the street the stranger resumes speaking, "I live on the other side of the river and come over here when new diggin' is goin' on and look for Indian relics. Bob Gavin's the name. Dad use to farm this land for the Comparet family fifty years ago. From your looks, I think you found more than just arrowheads."

"Mister, I don't know if we should show you this..."

"Quiet, Stan..." Nyle whispers.

"Ha! If you fellas found bones or skulls, don't think you are the first. My dad found plenty while tillin' the grounds around here and over by the Maumee. He simply dug a trench and threw 'em in there whenever he had to so he could continue plowin'."

"Really?" Nyle asks.

"I shouldn't tell ya this, but there was one fella my pop knew named Harrington, that lived up on Begue Street. He collected a bunch of skulls from around here and displayed them in his basement.

"Egad," reacts Stan.

"I don't know whatever happened to that collection, or him for that matter. Don't think I wanna know. Bones and graves and stuff like that back then, of early settlers, wasn't that big a deal, I guess."

Stan introduces his sibling and himself to the chatty Bob Gavin and states they are probably going to contact the sheriff and let him know what they found.

"You guys won't get in trouble," continues Gavin. "Older folks use to tell me these open fields use to be an old Indian village. On the other side of the St. Joe, where I live, was one, and on down the Maumee about two miles was another one, and up the St. Joe, a few hundred feet from here, was a British fort. Shoot, I'm startin' to ramble now. Sorry 'bout that fellas."

"No, that's alright," Nyle says shaking his head. "We're about done here for the day."

"In fact, we're gonna let somebody know 'bout this discovery right shortly," adds Stan.

"If ya want to use my telephone you can follow me over to my house," offers Bob.

"Thank you, Mr. Gavin. Stan, you want to go with our new friend here and I'll gather up what we got and finish things for the day."

"Alright," his brother says crawling out of the trench, "lead the way, Mr. Gavin."

As the two strolled, Bob Gavin asks, "You like history, Stan?"

"Yes I do."

"Some sort of battle took place around here. Ya know, the Miami didn't take too kindly of pioneers movin' in on their land. And for that matter, other Indian tribes comin' in, either. As you can tell from those bone markings you saw, it got kinda nasty."

"Yes, I agree. But I'll tell ya what, Mr. Gavin. It's a little weird but whenever I uncover something like the old bones here or an artifact while workin', I think to myself, if they could talk, I wonder what they'd have to say?"

Chapter 2

Late summer, 1790 - Ohio River, Marietta, Ohio

"Grab that sweeper oar on the starboard side, E.J.! Pay attention! You ain't gettin' no free ride down the river for nothin'. We gotta get this big ole flatboat away from that bank and get in that faster current out there," says big Mike Fink while waving his right arm, "before we get snagged or grounded on some sandbar or worse."

"Sorry, Mr. Fink," E.J. says while jumping up on top of the tiller house cabin of the twenty by forty foot rectangular broadhorn. "I got caught up in telling my friend good bye."

"I's don't care 'bout no pretty girlfriend of yours."

"Charlotte's not my girlfriend... but, mayb..."

"And quit callin' me Mr. Fink! Criminy, I'm only a few years older than you. Call me Mike or Big Mike or King of the River! Ha!" he roars with a slight smile.

"King of the Bull, might be a better name." E.J. responds.

"Hope you's trying to be funny, little man," retorts Fink.

"Heck no, Mr. Mike. When you rode that long horned cow yesterday in front of all those people and stayed on him 'til he calmed down, why that was amazing. He was buckin' and trying to toss you into kingdom come! How'd you do that and why would you wanna do that?"

"Oh, that was nothin' and besides a lot of those people watchin' bet a lot of money I couldn't do it. That was just fun to me, and I made a few bucks. Besides, if you build a little reputation people respect ya more. Why, you wait. You ain't seen nothin' yet. Why, I can out run, out jump, out wrestle about anybody along this river. Got some real God given talent.

"Hey, your uncle Ike is real good with that long pole keepin' us away from that fallen tree there. Maybe you two wanna stay with me and my business instead of getting off at Lousantiville."

"Nope, helpin' steer this big boat is kinda fun and all, but like I told you back at Fort Pitt, we signed on to General Harmar's army. Unk and I are even more determined after being around the other militia from Pennsylvania back there at Fort Harmar.

"It's a tragedy what them renegade Injuns have done to the farmers and settlers in western Pennsylvania and we's gonna wreak some revenge for them and for my Uncle Ike's family bein' taken from him.

"It was bloody awful. Uncle Isaac still won't talk about it and it's been a good two years since it happened."

"Well, I hope you two are good fighters cause all I seen loadin' up back there at Marietta was a bunch of old men and young boys with broken squirrel shooters. Why, that's a recipe for no good."

"Uncle Ike thinks we will be rewarded with some free land from our new government after we whip them redskins. At least that's what Mr. Bashorn, the militia recruiter, thought would happen. Guys in the Revolutionary war got some free acres as prize. Besides that, we're getting six whole dollars for only two months adventure.

"Uncle Isaac wants to start over out here."

"Me? It's time to move on. It got too crowded in the cabin with ma and pa and younger brothers and sisters. Besides, I'm almost fifteen."

"Fifteen? Why, that's about the age I started doin' this river boatin' stuff. Hey, we makin' good time out in this fast current. That rain a couple nights ago brought the river up. Gotta look for those underwater snags though, they can be a real problem if you ain't watchin'."

"I'm watchin', Mike," says E,J.

"We also gotta stay to the Virginia side if we can. The Indian war parties from up north have been comin' down here and attacking flatboats, crossin' into Kentucky county, stealin' horses, hurtin' settlers and takin' some captive. Ever since Harmar been organizing this army of his and stopped patrolin' the Ohio side of the river with his rangers, the varmints been more brave about makin' raids. I'd like to think we's gonna be alright. We got about twenty troops and such on this boat alone and there is at least twenty big flatboats following us, loaded down with militia from Penn and volunteers from along these parts."

"Yeah, there is a bunch back there," confirms E.J.

"Horses, beefs, flour, whiskey and corn, you name it, we bringin' it," brags Mike Fink.

As the day winds down and darkness starts casting a shadow over the river valley full of beech, birch and buckeye trees, the flatboat entourage floats to the Kentucky side of the 300 yard wide Ohio River to set up camp for the night. Fink, all six feet three inches of self-proclaimed raw muscle, seeks a previous camp site so there is a proven access to the bank.

It takes an hour to get the flatboats tied up along the shore, tents put up and fires going for the night.

Isaac Carlisle brings his nephew and the two boys they befriended back up river three days ago, together and gives instructions. "Ben, it's your turn to take the first watch tonight, then E.J.. Bobby till about three o'clock. I'll finish up till day break. Make sure your musket is primed and stay awake! There is a lot of folks in this camp here so we should be okay. But the farther we go down river and away from Fort Pitt and Fort Harmar the more dangerous it's gonna be with warrior parties."

"Yeah, well, Fink was tellin' some real whopper stories today, so I don't know how scared I gotta be," informs E.J.

"We'll be beddin' down right in here," says Uncle Isaac. "Look around, boys. Remember what it looks like so you don't go disturbin' people in the middle of the night and scarin' 'em. Okay? Let's go report to Fink. He'll assign our spot tonight as he has been."

E.J., while glancing around for Charlotte, walks with his uncle and the new friends he had made, through the camp to Mike Fink's meeting place listening to campers laughing, joking and talking about pretty much an uneventful day. Some people with fiddles or banjos serenade the campfires with an occasional light dance step now and then and pretty good singing voices cutting through.

"Who the heck told you how to lead an army?" bellowed the Kentucky militia Major James McMillin, appointed to escort the Pennsylvanians down the river. "Harmar wants me to lead this battalion. Didn't you get the memo back at Marietta when I got aboard the flatboat tied up behind ya?"

"Major, you got no memo that I seen. It's my armada and I'm callin' the shots till we get to Losantiville in a few days!" responds Mike Fink. "And whatta you gonna do about it?"

"I don't care if you are a dang bull rider. Why, anybody with any common sense wouldn't have even tried that! Besides, you ain't no military guy!"

"You call this military? All I see is a bunch a women folks washin' their woolseys!"

"Why you big lug young snot nose," answers McMillin with an off balanced swing at Fink, "You don't know nothing!"

Mike ducks the Major's fist and with one quick swoop picks the slightly portly officer, up over his head. Walks him a few steps to the riverbank and tosses the Major into the murky water of the Ohio.

The young impressionable Pennsylvania boys with gaping mouths wide-open, stand there in amazement. The resulting splash raises a loud laughter from all those observing the disagreement and causes the startled horses tied up to the high line nearby to rear up slightly.

After stifling his amusement, Fink offers a hand to the sputtering McMillin to help him up out of the chest high water.

"Thanks," responds the militia leader as he grabs hold of Fink's outstretched hand. But with a quick yank by the Major, Big Mike goes head over heels into the drink creating even a bigger splash and louder laugh by an even larger crowd witnessing the event.

"Now, as I was gonna say," begins Major McMillin pulling himself out of the river, "here is where you will be stationed. In fact, some men led by Major Paul are already out there on watch. We cannot take any chances. I cannot emphasize it more to you raw recruits, you ain't in some comfy fort. I guarantee the redskins are out there watching and will take your hair if they get a chance and will be gone before you're dead."

The night on the Ohio River went by quietly. Camp breaks and Mike Fink's flatboat, loaded with their cargo, pushes off from the bank first, with the rest of the flatboats following.

"Mr. Mike, can I ask you something?" inquires E.J.

"Ha, you wanna ask me about that fun last night, don't ya?"

"Fun?"

"I was a bit out of character wasn't I? Hey, I had to let the Major come out best. He's gonna lead you soldieries into some bad situations at Miamitown, if you's even get there. Don't ya know that's the heart of Injun land? Well, the Major, he needs all the respect he can get right now. Guys who know me understand. The rest saw what I did to him and coulda done to him if I wanted. Besides, I got future bets I got to set up. Ha!"

"Hey, Fink! Where'd the other boats go?" asks Uncle Isaac from his pole position.

"Dang, this may not be good," answers Mike. "They must a got snagged in that narrow current back there. We got ourselves through it and I assumed it would be no problem for dem. This is not good. The current is slowin' a bit and we can't be seen cause of the bend in the river we just went around."

"What's the problem? Just shore up and wait for 'em," E.J. offers.

"Hold it! Idle fellows with them poles", he yells to the six men on each side of the flatboat. Maybe the rest of the boats be comin' real quick."

"What's that in the water?" one of E.J.'s new friends, Bobby Fulton, asks. "Looks like blankets over there snagged in the water? Over by them rocks, Mr. Fink."

"Bodies. Them's bodies, kid!" cries Fink. "We may have... Yep, here they come," the flatboat leader states while pointing to the Ohio side of the river. "I've never seen 'em come out of Raccoon Creek before!"

Seven canoes full of black and red war painted Shawnee Indians paddle as hard as they can toward Mike Fink's flatboat. Each of the warriors in the canoes brandish a light weight hunting musket, sheathed scalping knife and a tomahawk clinging to their waist.

"Grab your guns and weapons. We in for somethin'!" barks Mike Fink as he hangs onto the long sweeper directing the barge toward the Kentucky side of the river. Ducking behind the sideboard that surrounds the top of the tiller house roof, he shouts, "You down below! Open up your slide windows and get ready to shoot! They ain't expectin' ten militia guns roaring back at 'em from inside the cabin!

"Get on the other side of the cabin E.J.! Grab your gun! You guys on the starboard side, drop dem poles and get over on the other side! What the heck you thinkin'? Get over there!"

Soon after Mike Fink's alarming orders, Indian musket balls strike the wood structure and whiz by heads and bodies. Two of the older pole men scrambling to get to cover are struck and fall overboard floating lifelessly with the current alongside the craft.

"Over here, E.J.!" hollers Uncle Isaac. "Stay down and take steady aim over the sideboard. Ben, you too, take a look, fire on command and reload quickly! Where's Bobby?"

"He went in to get his rifle," reports E.J.

The Shawnees start whooping loudly and more confidently as they close in. Then, the war party slows with a panic look as they see several muskets peering out at them through the port holes and windows.

"Let 'em have it, boys!" orders Fink.

Poor shooting and misfires scare the Indians more than kill any. Not anticipating such an arsenal, the Shawnee turn around. The trailing flatboats, finally dislodged, observe what is going on and hurriedly, pushing with the poles where it is shallow enough, close the gap.

The war painted Shawnees canoe away from the intended target, knowing the odds will be better to attack the river traffic at another time.

A few pot shots, from long distance, by the boat militia have a scant chance of hitting anything but it did settle nerves and take out frustration of losing two comrades.

Smoke from ignited flintlocks bellow out of the flatboat cabin that is used to prevent the weather elements from ruining the dry good supplies. But this time it served as a floating fortress.

Bobby comes out of the shelter choking and coughing with several other men and women, "I can hardly breathe, can't see or hear nothin' now, dad burnit."

"Good thing the rest of the boats started catchin' up," laments Uncle Isaac, "cause we aren't much of a fightin' crew."

"I tend to agree, Ike," remarks Fink. "Fellas, let's get our two friends out of the water. Anybody else get harmed? Any injuries?" Fink asks, staring at an arm and hand wound on two militia. "Let's get 'em taken care of. Ladies, couple guys there. Can you help 'em? Thanks."

"The shootin' and weapons gotta get better," moans Uncle Isaac again. "And look at that, will ya? Those fools on that flatboat back there. What are they doin' tryin' to catch those Injuns?"

"Waste a time," finishes Fink, "and it could get 'em killed."

"We got two beeves struggling back here," informs the frontier hardened Mrs. Thacker. "The side board corral came in handy protectin' most of them, though."

"Ok, have someone put 'em down," orders Fink. "We'll butcher 'em for sup' later tonight."

"The two fellas we lost have kin back up at Redstone near Fort Pitt," Uncle Isaac informs everyone. "But we'll have to bury them tonight along with the two victims they're unsnagging in the water."

The next couple days see heavy rains swelling the tributaries leading to the Ohio River and again speeding up the current.

Signs of Indian attacks and more atrocities are seen along the shores as well as bloated dead animals and humans caught on something or floating in the water.

E.J.'s flatboat and several others witness twenty five hollering Kentuckians on horseback. They were crossing a ford in the river from Ohio back into Virginia that many call Kentucky, waving the scalps of Native Americans. The militia and women folk cheer, but a new sense of concern begins to well up.

Approaching Limestone Landing also known as Maysville, on the Virginia side of the Ohio River, the boats anchor for the night. Supplies are dropped off and picked up. Some passengers not with the militia will make this town their home or go on to Kenton Station, about three miles inland from the river. Daniel Boone and Simon Kenton, frontier legends and founders of a tavern and settlement near the water highway, make people feel somewhat safer establishing in this community. Beautiful forested hillsides overlooking the Ohio on both sides of the river make a picturesque place to settle. What was unsettling was the news Major McMillin brought to everyone.

"I thought I made it clear to you people not to fall for Indian tricks and traps along the river. Report is two of the last three boats in our flotilla got lured toward the Ohio side by some red haired boy yelling for help. As they got close to shore to rescue the kid the savages attacked, slayed most, captured some.

"We'll try to tell the rangers and government scouts 'bout it but truth is, not much patrolling along the river is goin' on cause of the army build up at Fort Washington. From what I've heard, Governor St. Clair gave Harmar a tight budget and Harmar can't afford to hire more rangers. Besides, both are sticklers 'bout money as we have found out the last six years in this territory."

"Uncle Isaac, I gotta find Charlotte. I hope she wasn't on one of those last couple flatboats."

"I'll search with ya, E.J. All the boats are in, so her and her family have to be 'round here close by this landing, preparin' to have supper."

It didn't take long to find the fifteen year old, long blond haired girl and her family.

"We knew people on those boats, E.J," Charlotte softly speaks, sobbing. They were the nicest folks you'd ever wanna meet. They'd do anything for ya."

"I kinda understand, Charlotte. Uncle Ike here lost some family... well. Ya know. It's tough."

"Why do people keep comin' down this river?" asks Charlotte.

"I don't know for sure," answers E.J. "Maybe, well maybe, it's a callin' or the spirit of freedom after years of those dang British tellin' folks what to do."

"Father says we are goin' on. We've come this far and we're obligated to General Harmar. We're not goin' back."

"Charlotte, we are too. We're campin' over yonder," pointing toward Ben and Bobby two campfires away. "If you need anything, don't hesitate to come see us, okay?"

Ike and E.J. make their way to Bobby and Ben's set up, just in time to hear another warning.

"It could get a little crazy tonight," informs Mike Fink talking loudly so anyone could here. "They's a lot of unlawfulness, and ya throw in whiskey and rum at Boone's tavern and ya neva knows what's gonna happen."

"Did I hear my name?" Daniel Boone says, walking up with his ten year old son, Nathan. "You all listenin' to this river king? How ya doin' folks? I just wanta add that Injuns are out there more than ever lately, if ya don't already know. You be careful goin' into these here forests to gather campfire wood or relieve yourselves. Why the surveyor of this here territory, John May, got killed back upriver last March. Don't want to scare ya, just wanna make you wiser."

"Thanks, Dan'el," says Fink. "So protect yourselves and mind your own business. With a coupla more days we get you all to Losantiville, er, I mean. What did I just hear they call it now? Cincinnati, that's it, Cincinnati."

Chapter 3

Summer, 1790 - Kekionga, Future Lakeside area, Fort Wayne, Indiana

"Look at that Indian boy whip that ball!" exclaims Henry Hay, one of the few British residents at the confluence of the St. Joseph and St. Mary's Rivers.

"He reminds me of Little Turtle a few years ago," replies his French companion, Antoine Lasselle. "Running Deer dominates the games around here whenever competition takes place. Injuns love their fun."

"What are they playing?"

In his broken English, Lasselle explains. "The Delaware introduced it while you were in Detroit. As you can see they have goals at each end of the field to fling the ball into. I don't know what they call that stick and basket attached to it but they can't use their hands to throw it."

"It looks a little rough," Hay says wincing. "They are good sports about it, though. With all the corn planted around here I'm amazed they found a playing area. I'm even more surprised the squaws allow their daughters, as young as they are, to play this game."

"Morning Bird does a good job out there and competes as well as anyone of them," compliments Lasselle. "Besides, interacting with the boys from different clans sets up future marriages."

"Well, I have to get back over to Frenchtown. Ha. You must like that," chides Hay. "An Englishmen heading over to Frenchtown."

"Don't matter to me," Lasselle says grinning. "Plenty of business for everyone."

"Some tribes comin' haven't been here in a while and Kizer is by himself over there manning the post. Some'll take advantage of him if I don't get back to help."

Running Deer, carrying the ball in his lacrosse stick, sprints past and around two Delaware tribesmen and Morning Bird, scoring by hurling it past the keeper so powerfully it rips through the weaved canes and reeds in the back of the goal, flying over a blackberry patch and bounding into the Maumee River nearby.

"Hold up, Mr. Lasselle!" yells Running Deer racing toward the two traders while the awestruck participants fetch the ball out of the leisurely flowing current. The breech bottomed nearly fifteen year old Indian kid asks in Lasselle's native tongue, "did you get the Fusil De Chasse musket in yet?"

"Can you believe it, my friend, almost perfect French coming out of such a young Miami boy?" Turning to the Indian, "They should be coming in any day now, Running Deer. And if I don't get them in soon maybe Mr. Hay, here, will. By the way, Hay, that means hunting gun." Turning back to Running Deer, "You know what it will cost, don't ya son?"

"I'm getting closer to the amount of furs you want. I should be out there checking my traps now but couldn't resist showing off to those Wea and Piankeshaw," glancing at them, "over there watching our new game."

"Yes, you're doing good," Lasselle praises. "You are very close to being a brave."

"Tecumseh just got into our village yesterday. He will be taking several of us younger ones out tomorrow for war training which usually leads to bringing back some game if we're fortunate."

"Oh, you will be," Lasselle says confidently.

As the three walked on, the conversation turns more serious. "Rumors are coming true, aren't they?" asks Hay.

"'Fraid so," the French trader agrees. "The Americans are organizing an army of sorts down at Losantiville on the Ohio."

"Blue Jacket and Little Turtle will be coming in soon," rattles off Running Deer excitedly as he picks up the pace to stay with the white men. "They'll be coming back from a raid into our hunting grounds south of the Ohio River."

"I caught some of that," utters Hay. "Doesn't this lad know English?"

"In fact, I do, Mr. Hay. I thought you knew French," discloses Running Deer smiling.

"Ha! Well, not as good as you," Hay responds shaking his head in amazement. "Little Turtle, I'm sure, will hold a meeting when he gets back, Running Deer. And by the way, Running Deer, you will be very good at whatever you do."

As the two bid goodbye to the young Indian, the Frenchman and Englishman walk by the gardens, near the three river confluence, planted with squash, pumpkins and beans.

Three distinct separate Indian villages lay east to west; Delaware, Shawnee and the Miami.

"To be honest, I don't like this particular section of Kekionga, Frenchy," Hay says as they stroll silently west toward the St. Joseph River trying not to glance at the seven forlorn Americans held captive near the shelter they stay in. A pole, with ashes surrounding it, stands thirty yards away and acts as a constant reminder of what might be in store for the prisoners.

Approaching the two white men, the Shawnee warrior Tecumseh, with American scalps attached to his waist, nods at them. Next to him, Miami Chief Richardville walks by looking straight ahead, ignoring the two traders.

"I know Richardville likes your countrymen, Lasselle," Hay says glancing back. "His family has dealt with the French for a hundred years or so, but he is still upset the British defeated yours in the French and Indian War.

"But add to it my country then losing the war against the American colonists, just adds to his animosity."

"Speaking of dislike," says Lasselle as the trader friends ford the shallow St. Joseph River westerly to Frenchtown or sometimes called

LeGris' village, "Chief Legris better not see these Potawatomi and Wea trading with Kinzie."

"Oh, that will be somethin'," Hay says smiling. "'specially after Legris caught them huntin' up by Cedar Creek last winter."

"Then again, it might be okay" reconsiders Lasselle and then finishing his thought, "Ya know, Little Turtle will probably need all the help he can get against Gen'ral Harmar soon."

Sunday morning, the next day, three French boys run around amongst the cabins, wigwams and surprisingly modernistic houses of Kekionga ringing cattlebells and calling people to the morning's service.

Father Louis Payet, the local priest from Montreal, is hosting Catholic Mass in one of only a few larger frame houses in the French and Miami village. This one is owned by Mr. Barthelmis, the oldest known white resident of the community.

"Mornin', Mr. and Mrs. Adamher, Mr.Dufresnes, hello Mr. Hay. Did you bring your flute today, and Mr. Kinzie, welcome, how about your fiddle?"

Both nod affirmatively. "Gotta little hangover though. Sorry, Father," apologizes the lean five foot eight inch Englishman, John Kinzie, from Quebec, Canada.

"I can see that," Father Louis acknowledges. "We'll try to cure you of that today. Ha!"

"You just want us here for our music," muses Hay. "Don't ya fatha?"

"No, just your faith," he wisecracks laughing. "The music you bring is a gift from God."

"I'm impressed by the trappers and traders along with the few Indians living up and down the rivers that come every Sabbath day," Hay compliments. "A lot of 'em, well, some of them out there are pretty rough characters."

After the service was over, food and drink is served and Hay takes out his flute and Kinzie his fiddle for sing-a-longs and some ladies and gentlemen join in with impromptu, classy dancing.

Three miles north, up the St. Joe trail from Kekionga, Tecumseh is working with future warriors.

"Flip him with your back foot and bring your elbow to his head. Good, Long Snake!" praises the adult warrior from the Ohio country. "Come here, all of you. Come up close to listen to me. You all must be quick, fast and agile. That is what will make you difficult to defeat. But working in unison is the key to victory. A single stick snaps, but the bundle of sticks is strong."

The young Miami have been practicing in an open meadow near the St. Joe trail north of Kekionga, evidenced by the scattered trees with tomahawks and arrows stuck in them from practice earlier in the day.

"Gather your weapons, gather your weapons, young ones. Okay, Running Deer you go out and around like I told you. It is good to see you have the dirt and clay striped on your face. You others do the same. We want to blend in like Manitou nature wants you to. Everyone has obtained their Manitou, right? Some, not yet? It won't be long. Must reach puberty. Young squaws, too. If you haven't been prepared yet, let me tell you."

Tecumseh kneels down on one knee and has the others do the same in a semi-circle in front of him and begins.

"You will be sent into the forest by your father or your mother, or the Shaman, or the chief of your clan, whoever, with no food or weapon. There is no eating. You must stay in isolation, sleep until Kitchi Manitou with power from the all-powerful delivers your personal Manitou in a dream. Obtaining it is very special, you will know when it happens.

Your Manitou becomes your guardian spirit of whom you must make sacrifices and be respectful. If after two or three days you do not obtain Manitou you will try again at a later time. You who have Manitou know what I am speaking of.

But to be truly considered a brave you must go on a war party. Let us prepare for that."

The boys wearing headbands with two or three feathers around their Mohawk cuts or hairless skulls smear their face, arms and legs with soil and clay. The male décor helps them blend in with nature whether they are hunting or in a war party.

Tecumseh continues teaching and re-teaching, "Fan out, ten each way from me, eight paces between each one of you, remember?"

The legend-to-be instructor continues. "Pay attention to my hands and fingers as has been previously instructed. We will move as a line easterly away from river, practicing swift and slow movements staying low with eye contact forward and toward me, head on a pivot. Move smoothly in order to blend in with nature.

"Running Deer will have his reward soon."

As the line moves, silently stopping, moving diagonally left and right in unison slowly and then quickly, the patient Tecumseh flickers his fingers from his out stretched arms. The youngsters on the ends move out more swiftly and low to the ground to form a human semi-circle.

Ahead, the grazing white tail deer sense something and look up gazing, unsure of the encroachment taking place. A ten point buck reacting to the sudden rise of the young Indians kicks up and jumps away from the Miami youngsters in a full bounding sprint. The three doe, with the buck, take off in different directions.

Running Deer, spotting the antlered male, slowly rises up from his hiding place the deer is heading for. Calmly, he aims his man size bow, pulls back the string and releases an arrow piercing the buck cleanly through the heart, bringing down the proud white tail, immediately.

"Wahoo wa wa, Wahoo, ayh yi yi," the young Indians race toward Running Deer to congratulate him and then break into a victory dance around the fallen buck, celebrating the unit's achievement.

"Very good, very good," Tecumseh compliments them humbly.

A few days later, in Kekionga, outside the cabin of Morning Bird, her mother asks the visiting trader John Kinzie, "What you give us for these beautiful blankets, rugs, leggings, skirts, Mr. Kinzie? They are highly decorative as you can see. The beads are very colorful. Make us deal, Kinzie."

"Well, now, they are some of the best I've seen you ladies make," John Kinzie replies. "Running Deer, come over here, will you?"

"Yes, Mr. Kinzie?" Running Deer curiously asks.

"Help Morning Bird bring the handsome tapestries and clothing these ladies have made over to my post, will you? I also have a new batch of trade guns that just came in on the last pirogue from Detroit."

"Morning Bird," suggests Running Deer, "let's take them over in my canoe. The rain last night brought the river up. I need to pass by my home first, though, to tell my father about the muskets, okay?"

"Anything you say, Running Deer."

As Running Deer and Morning Bird unload the canoe in Frenchtown, the future brave breaks the silence, "Kekionga sure seems busier with a lot more people. It is about double the 500 that live here most of time."

"I agree," says Morning Bird, "and by the way, thanks for your kind help."

Morning Bird slowly turns her head eyeing the villages across the river and observingly says, "I sense something is going to..."

All activities in the French and Miami side of the river come to a halt. Everyone's attention gazes east toward the Maumee River, 1000 yards away. Riding captured horses from American settlers bare back across the deepened river, yelping, is a posse of twelve Shawnees. Led by Shawnee Chief Blue Jacket, they also bring in white pioneers against their will. Coming up on shore and riding toward the other American captives, they stop a hundred yards away from the torture pole.

"Here we go again," Lasselle says speaking in French walking up from behind to help Morning Bird and Running Deer unload. "Seems like we're seeing more of this lately."

Young and old braves, squaws and children grab hickory sticks, willow branches and clubs and form two parallel lines for the new prisoners to run between.

"Aren't you going to join them?" asks Lasselle.

"No more," says Running Deer frowning. "We found out at the last calumet dance, didn't we Morning Bird? Each of our own Manitou discourages cruelty and emboldens us to only defend ourselves and our land."

"The young ones think it is a game," expresses Morning Bird. "But when they get older they will either have good, evil or neutral Manitou to advise them."

Three men and a woman are yanked off their horses and are instructed by a chief in charge of the apprehended settlers on how to run the gauntlet.

The youngsters stand on both sides at the front with sticks and switches. The women are next with larger sticks and the men finish the tunnel with war weapons.

As the first settler is prepared to run, walk, crawl or die trying to get through the 50 yard long torturous path, Blue Jacket and the other warriors who had just returned from their venture along the Ohio, take the captured horses and ponies to the corral. They know the yelling and screaming would be unnerving to them.

"Let's deliver Morning Bird and her mother's items," suggests Lasselle, "to Kinzie and look at those muskets. What do you say, you two?"

CHAPTER 4

Mid-September, 1790 - Cincinnati, Ohio

"There it is, E.J., up yonder, your destination is here. Fort Washington."

"Yep, I see it. But first, let me get this straight. Is Bobby Fulton tellin' me the truth, Mr. Mike? Did you really shoot that mug full of whiskey off the top of Danny William's head back there at Boone's tavern in Limestone, from fifty paces?"

"Actually it was rum. But, well, now, ya know I'm a dang good shot, have a good musket and Danny stood real still, even though he had a couple, ya know. Ha! Fifty paces, huh?"

"Yeah, fifty!" exclaims E.J.

"Boy that story is sure gettin' bigger. I got a little extra coin jingling, too. But I ain't braggin'. Why, I'd get knocked on da head by some stranger," declares Fink.

The riverbanks of the Ohio in front of Fort Washington are lined with abandoned wooden water craft of every size with a few on the Kentucky side.

"What's with all the boats?" inquires Ben Conrad from his pole position on the starboard side.

"Some not being used anymore," Mike explains, "Many of 'em will be sold, taken apart for buildin' houses, barns, corrals, sheds, outhouses, wagons, beds, anythin' imaginable in the new settlement and fort here."

Supplies and animals are carried and led off the flatboats by the militia and settlers.

Some frontiersmen are loading the vessels with goods that continue to take pioneers on downstream. The Mississippi River and eventually New Orleans, near the Gulf of Mexico, will end a trip for flatboat people wanting to go that far.

As Fink prepares to leave, he wishes E.J., Uncle Ike, Bobby and Ben good luck.

"I thought I was to take Major Hamtramck and part of his army on down to the Wabash and up to Vincennes, but I guess they left last month. I still got a good load though.

"You guys'll be okay. I was talkin' to one of the scouts goin' on your journey, Daniel Williams himself, back up river. As a part time scout myself, well, he sounds like he knows the territory and what he's doin'. Daniel, along with that guy," as he points to a tall man in a long black coat and wide brimmed hat, taking long strides up the bank toward the fort carrying a book, "why, you be even better off. Ha! So long!"

As E.J., Uncle Isaac, Bobby and Ben walk up the slightly sloped bank along with the other 350 Pennsylvania militia and camp followers toward the main gate of the fort, E.J. remarks. "Now I know why we're called militia."

Bobby, impressed also, chimes in, "Look at those straight lines they are marchin' in and the blue coats and white pants they are wearin'. Why, they even got round fancy hats."

"Don't worry fellas they'll train us just like them," consoles Uncle Isaac.

The Pennsylvania militia commanding officer, Lieutenant Colonel Truby, leading the way, overhears Uncle Isaac and responds, "I hope you're right, Carlisle, but we won't have any fancy uniform like that. It's buckskins and a coonskin hat for some of us. Others, just plain woolseys and what we got on our heads."

A few strides farther Bobby exclaims, "Look at the size of these fort walls and the blockhouses at each corner sittin' up there nice and pretty! I'm gonna feel safe in there."

At the fort's front gate, greeting the Pennsylvania force was Lieutenant Ebenezer Denny, Major John Whistler and Private John Smith.

Denny eyes the raw recruits and the camp followers made up of women and children, with a long gaze and stare, with very little expression, then states, "I see you have a few horses and some tents. We'll find out about the weapon situation in the next few days. You'll be camping on the east side of the fort."

"Not inside, officer?" Truby asks.

"Don't worry, you'll come in if we're attacked but the savages around here have been pretty intimidated by what they been spyin'. Have some sentries out though just in case. We'll have guards in the blockhouses over lookin', too. How was your trip down river from Fort Pitt? Is it Colonel Truby?" Denny asks as he looks down at an official roster.

"Actually, it is Lieutenant Colonel Christopher Truby. We got attacked and lost some people as well as some supplies and animals. Major McMillin and Mike Fink got the vast majority of us here okay."

"Treat your horses to what we have at the corral in back and report to the headquarters inside at 9 A.M. tomorrow. Private John Smith will help you get settled. Good day, sir."

"A private? I think we deserve a little more respect than that," says Truby.

"Hey, give me a break, Lieutenant. I just got a promotion, so follow me," Smith counters as he winks at Denny.

"Man," E.J. speaks, leaning toward his buddies standing near him, "I can't hear or know what Truby and that fancy lookin' officer is talkin' about, but from what I see here, the Injuns are going to be scared of what's comin' at 'em."

"Yeah, easy money, too. I think the toughest part was just getting down the river to here." Bobby gloats.

"I sure hope so," Ben expresses hesitantly.

A few days go by as the Pennsylvania militia trains in martial arts, have hand to hand instruction on fighting with their side weapons, and practice loading and firing what few muskets and pistols the force brought along that work.

The fort is more like a factory, as men and women fix equipment and firearms to make them functional.

"We are a little thin in the cavalry that we are supposed to supply from Pennsylvania," Major Paul says approaching the three boys and Uncle Ike. "I just got three horses from the military corral. You guys have any riding experience?"

Amazingly, all four former farmers chirp, "Yes, sir", at the same time.

"Here ya go," enlightens Private Smith following Paul bringing three mares by the reins up to them. "I got three sabers, also. Now don't go cutting yo' hands off. Ha!"

After each shows Major Paul they could ride, Major Fontaine, in charge of the Cavalry unit, rides up after observing the new prospects from a distance. He offers a mini lesson on the use of the curved sword.

"Alright, let's see what ya got," commands Paul. "Ride to the post down there that has a fresh gourd Smith just put on top of and lop it off. Each take a turn and ride back hard, dadgumit."

After the tryout ends, E.J. makes the decision easy. "Fellas, I'm gonna stay on the ground. I like my odds better with my musket, tomahawk and maybe a bayonet, if they ever arrive."

More necessities including guns, kettles for cooking and tents are anxiously being waited on to come down the river. The 575 or so pack horses and mules needed to carry the gear and pull the three brass cannons had been steadily coming in all summer. One thing that was overdue and causing General Josiah Harmar some consternation was the approximately 800 Kentucky militia of Virginia which Colonel John Hardin was to deliver.

"I don't get it, Major Whistler. I'm more anxious now than when I was at Valley Forge in the winter during the war. We have to get movin'. It's gonna get cold sooner up north and we're two weeks away from Kekionga," Harmar laments pacing in the southwest blockhouse overlooking the river.

"We just had a couple hundred Kentuckians with us on the trial run up the Ohio to the Scioto River and back, and other than mistakenly killin' a few friendly Indians it went well, I thought. And dadburnit, they were just supposed to go back home, kiss their families, and get back here."

Below that same blockhouse, E.J. and others are trying to fit the new bayonets on their French made Charleville musket when a cry goes out from the blockhouse at the other corner of the fort.

"There they are, sir," says the guard as an arm extends out pointing, "fording the river near the Licking River mouth!"

"Alright, that's good, finally. But they may have to swim their horses and selves a little, for the rivers up a bit right now. Hope they keep their gunpowder ammo dry. We are somewhat short on that. Dang, they should have got on a flatboat up stream."

"At least they are here," says Whistler inserting some optimism.

"Private Smith!" Harmar calls out watching the new arrivals.

"Yes, sa'."

"Attend Major Ziegler at the front gate to get the Kentucky militia settled in on the west side. Also, inform Ziegler I need to see Colonel Hardin up here as soon as he gets off his horse."

Right away, sa'."

"Whistler, my friend, we could use a drink."

As the Virginia/Kentuckians whip their horses riding the path up the bank from the river crossing, Uncle Isaac asks the young boys in amusement, "What do we have here?"

Galloping hard and fast on saddled horseback are several militia from Hardin's command whooping and hollering, circling the fortress, riding through troops and fort workers and then pulling up to the front gate with their steeds panting and snorting. "Ha," declares one of them,

"I knew we could beat that ole Hardin here! Where's the refreshments? Yee ha!"

A couple nights later on the east side of Fort Washington, rest is difficult to get.

"Man, I can't sleep again tonight, fellas, it's way too noisy," E.J. remarks. "It reminds me of Limestone. I gotta get up and stretch."

"Geez, there's regulars carryin' on again too, over in the town," Bobby says looking around rubbing his eyes. "Ha. Look at that Ben, in the back of the tent there sleepin' through all this. That bayonet charge practice today musta wore him out plenty."

"I think the Kentucky boys brought plenty of moonshine and are sharin' it with the soldiers," uttered Uncle Isaac. "I see a few of our garrison with' em, also."

The next day, E.J. wanders through camp after some morning marching, locates Charlotte, and starts some small talk. "We are going to be leavin' soon, Charlotte. I think we are ready but I don't know 'bout them boys from across the river."

"Mom talked to some ladies in their camp yesterday and they said they got some good fighters but they are concerned. No Simon Kenton and no Dan'l Boone joinin' us with their crowd."

"No Boone or Kenton?" asks E.J. "Shoot, I thought they were here already."

"Nope, they don't trust the General and would rather do their own raids into Ohio. They don't like following the beat of a drummer boy and taking orders, they say. Most of the 800 or so militia that came are made up of older, younger and substitutes."

"Substitutes? Oh yeah, we got some of those, too. They are gettin' payed to take somebody's place." E.J. says, shaking his head. "Why, some of them didn't even bring a gun."

"Speakin' of guns, E.J., Pa's been busy training but thought, just to be safe, ma and I oughta learn how to load and fire. We met a Mrs.

Thacker who already knows how to handle a musket and she has offered to show us."

"Yeah, I know her. She was on our flatboat," E.J. says surprisingly.

"In fact, she has her own musket," Charlotte adds. "She'll be along helpin' with the cookin' for the army regulars once we get movin'."

"That's a good deal, Charlotte, maybe I can show ya something 'bout shootin', too."

"Okay," Charlotte says with a smile. "I've seen ya shoot. You're pretty good."

The next day, inside Fort Washington, meetings take place.

"I don't know what kind of reaction we're goin' to get when we get back after this campaign, Major Whistler, but free land for serving?" General Harmar says lowering his voice to a whisper. "I don't know how that rumor got started. Maybe it was by Bashorn's recruiting speech in Pennsylvania? I don't have any authority over that."

"Anyway, assemble the officers and their seconds to the courtyard."

Near the assembling militia and regular army officers were soldiers being disciplined for breaking rules the night before. Punishment is standing several hours with their head and arms pinned in stocks.

Glancing sheepishly at those being punished, E.J., Ike, Bobby and Ben pass by feeling honored to be among the group chosen to hear Harmar speak. Even though they lacked experience, Truby personally asked them because they showed leadership qualities.

During Harmar's speech, the General rambles on with details about the budget and time restraints and having to get going. He mentions not being able to wait any longer because Major Hamtramck is already moving up the Wabash River, to the west, as a diversionary force to draw Indians away from Kekionga.

E.J. and the other boys stand awestruck of Harmar, barely listening. After all, this General served in the Revolutionary War with George Washington and Nathaniel Greene. He met Ben Franklin and in turn was introduced to King Louis XVI and Marie Antoinette of France by Franklin, for crying out loud. The Quaker schooling history lessons the boys received in Pennsylvania, come streaming back to them.

"Therefore, this is what we do from here," Harmar continues. "Colonel Hardin, you and 300 militia will head north tomorrow and improve the Clark trail with lead scout, Daniel Williams. The rest of the army will depart four days from now and follow the path wide enough for the three artillery pieces and army to pass comfortably. Maybe more supplies will come in before we leave.

"Williams, you got anything you wanna say?"

"Yeah, don't mistake the scouts for the enemy."

As the officers calm down from yucking it up a little bit, he continues. "I'm serious, you gotta few slackjaws that neva been on this type of campaign before and they'll shoot at anything that moves when they get scared.

"I want ya to meet Johnny Dee standing next to me and the Iroquois Indian is Degataga."

Williams uses Indian sign language and speaks Algonquin to tell Degataga what he had just told everyone.

Degataga signs back to Williams.

"He says hello and that he is your friend. Get a good look at him. The Iroquois don't like the Miami. Their rivalry goes way back. We have some other spies too, that will be your eyes on the trail and in battle. You'll see 'em all before Hardin leaves tomorrow. That's all I gotta say."

Harmar speaks up, "Colonel Hardin, you and Colonel Trotter stick around. I want to talk to you two. If there are no questions, you are all dismissed."

CHAPTER 5

Mid-September 1790 - Kekionga, Future Fort Wayne, Indiana

BAM! The musket smoke plumes the air and the echoes bounce off the surrounding oaks, maples and walnut trees.

"Now, I must pull back firing striker to half cock and pour some gunpowder into flash pan and close it. Next, I pour the rest into end of musket barrel that is upright. Placing lead ball down the barrel, I use rammer to push paper and wadding cloth in as well. Pull the ram rod out and place back on barrel. Aim and shoot."

"I think you're getting it down, Running Deer," expresses Morning Bird.

"Mr. Hay says a British soldier will fire off three shots per minute in battle when well trained, sometimes four."

"Well, you're getting there."

"Let's go get the turkey and head back. Father will be pleased that the musket shot did not go to waste."

After gathering the wild fowl, Morning Bird and Running Deer exit the forest northeast of Kekionga. Heading back to Kekionga, they follow the Detroit trail that parallels the north side of the peaceful Maumee River between the Shawnee village, Chillicothe, two miles downstream, and the headwater. A French occupied pirogue carrying furs passes by heading upstream. The paddling occupants are chattering away in their native tongue that Running Deer picks up on.

"The ones talking in the boat," Running Deer interprets, "say they may not be coming here for a while. Trouble is brewing."

As the couple draw closer to the villages surrounded by acres of corn fields, loud whoops and hollers can be heard from two Miami Indians riding stolen settler horses across the Maumee ford and into Kekionga pronouncing to all who can hear them, "Little Turtle is arriving from successful raid on the American intruders! He is approaching! Come see what he brings!"

As the Delaware, Shawnee and Miami villagers move toward the war party crossing the river, Morning Bird and Running Deer notice a red haired white boy, older than them, leading Little Turtle on horseback, but he is not one of the prisoners. The captives follow, tethered and led by several Indians.

Little Turtle dismounts and informs those gathered, "Although it has been a successful raid, we sadly have lost two of our warriors from the Delaware nation that live upstream on the St. Mary's River." Pointing to the Delaware represented here at Kekionga, he asks them directly, "What do you want me to do with white captives?"

Chief Richardville, Little Turtle's nephew, steps forward, looking back at a speechless Chief La-Pa-Win-Soe whose emotions of anger and sadness begin to overwhelm him and says, "What unnecessary circumstances these white invaders keep bringing to our land. I do not want to cast judgement for our friends, the Delaware, to strike the Americans dead. That will be up to their village chief and family of lost ones that live on the Kettle River."

Tah-Cum-Wah, mother of Chief Richardville, addresses La-Pa-Win-Soe, "Come, my friend. We take the intruders we have here, courtesy of the Little Turtle war party, to the families of the dead loved ones. We are heading home anyway. Death or adoption awaits them," she angrily announces as she leads the captives and her Miami attendants to the canoes gathered along the St. Joseph, to paddle up the St. Mary's River.

"They would burn at the stake right now, right here if it were up to me," William Wells, the red headed, furture son-in-law of Little Turtle, yells in broken Miami Algonquin.

All the gathered, standing solemnly, with anger intensifying, hear Wells and erupt into hollering and whooping in agreement. Their emotions carry them to the white captives already being held in

Kekionga. Two are drug out of their shelter, beaten and their lives eliminated.

Later that afternoon, Little Turtle leads the returned members of the war party in a 'scalp dance' at the pow wow area of Kekionga. Hopping twice on one foot to the other in rhythm of beating drums and vocal chants, many watch in celebration of the scalps of the whites the tribesmen had brought back. While dancing, the scalps are swung around in the air at the end of a stick. Other scalps are swung by hand.

Father Louis Payet observes the dance from across the St. Joseph River while talking to Antoine Lasselle.

"Sadly, earthly souls that are being taken by both the Americans and the warriors is nothing to them."

"We are seeing an increase in this," says Lasselle, "and I am afraid our British friends here and in Detroit are more than partly responsible."

"How's that?" inquires Father Louis.

"Those American scalps being swung around bring good reward and encourage the unrest in the new American territory," answers Lasselle.

"Seems the British are not finished with the Americans even though they lost to them in a war seven years ago," Father Louis concludes.

The calumet dance takes over the Indian festivities and shifts to 'striking the pole.' Many more villagers including chiefs and squaws gather around the chanting sing song dancers. Running Deer and Morning Bird sit down in the large circle to hear the stories of bravery. Food has been eaten including some cannibalism.

The late afternoon draws to evening with a fire in the middle of the circle casting a silhouette of warriors shuffling and bowing up and down. Suddenly, Chiksika, the older brother of Tecumseh, slams his tomahawk into the pole sticking up in the middle of the dance area near the fire and the drum beat and dancing stops and dancers sit down.

Chiksika, the only one standing speaks in his Shawnee dialect. "My Manitou gave me great courage to climb on top of intruder's cabin in our hunting grounds across the Ohio into Kentucky. When the white man comes out to see what was going on above him, I jumped down on him. Although he had great strength his scalp is here!" As he holds up the hair still attached to the top of a white man's head, the gathering roars with approval.

Chiksika starts dancing and chanting again and the youngsters, warriors and squaws of all ages join him. The drum beats and other rhythmic instruments add to the powerful atmosphere.

Abruptly, William Wells in his Indian garb now, takes his turn by forcefully sticking his crimson tomahawk into the pole. His wife, Sweet Breeze, also known as Little Turtle's daughter along with others stop dancing and sit down to listen as Wells begins talking.

"I am standing along the beautiful river Ohio waving at flatboats of intruders floating by. Dressed like the white boy I used to be, I call for help in a youthful voice. My red hair lures the trusting Americans near to rescue me. I draw up my hidden musket and my fellow raiding party leaps from cover and opens fire with muskets and arrows. Many of the pack horses we bring back with American goods come from that boat. But most important come," as he holds up five scalps that were attached to his waist, "these!" waving them above his head.

Wild cheering echoes through the village, off of trees and carries up and down the rivers.

As the dancing goes on, Running Deer puffs some smoke from the calumet that has been passed to him. He turns to Morning Bird and speaks, "Here, you may try it," passing the decorative celebratory pipe to her.

As Running Deer coughs slightly, Morning Bird informs him, "My Manitou demands other ways of pleasing it, sorry," and passes it to the next tribal member sitting next to her in the huge circle.

On and on the pole dance continues until all the stories of bravery and strategies are told.

Later that evening, Running Deer walks Morning Bird to her home when she asks him, "The Americans will not continue to put up with the treatment our people are inflicting on them, will they? The bravery our warriors boast about sounds like cruelty to me."

"The cruelty goes back and forth, Morning Bird. Unspeakable things were done to a hundred peaceful, friendly Delaware at a village in northern Ohio near the Lake Erie not long ago. Other atrocities committed by the whites have taken place and continue in southern Ohio. Some of the survivors live among us here in Kekionga to get away from that. Now, I regret to say, a long knife from a fort named after the great American Chief, Washington, could be extending here"

A couple mornings later, Henry Hay opens the window of his trading post preparing for another busy day, and gazes out toward the slowly flowing waters of the St. Joseph River. Thinking of possibly fishing later in the afternoon, a menacing looking Indian face pops up in the window staring right back at him with a scalping knife between his teeth and smiling mouth.

"Ahhh! Dang you Little Turtle!" Hay says as he stumbles backwards over a stool he uses to reach high things, hitting the back of his head on the floor. "You and your practical jokes! You are joking, right?"

"Of course, my fine Englishman friend. You are easy to fool with and besides, the muskets you have will be coming in handy soon I am afraid. Do you have bayonets, too?"

Hay rubbing the back of his head gets up and answers, "Maybe for your friends but not you after all the jokes you pull on me."

"Hmmm, maybe I'm not joking anymore."

Laughing, Hay responds, "Okay, okay, there will be one for you when they come in."

"By the way, Hay," Little Turtle asks, "how you like living in this Legris village part of Kekionga? You are treated right by the French?"

"Yes, hard to believe all the many nice houses and furnishings with multiple rooms intermixed among the wigwams."

"Ha. You should come visit my house," brags Little Turtle.

"The families and citizens living here so far away from the main population of their people are very easy to get along with. The lady friends Kinzie and I have met are a pleasure to entertain with the flute and fiddle we can play. Of course, as you know the flood last winter made things difficult around here for a while."

"Good to hear you like it here and of course the floods happen occasionally, but makes the land fertile for growing."

Little Turtle leans on the window sill and speaks softly, "There is big meeting coming up. I want you to know what is going on. You be there, okay?"

"Wouldn't miss it, Chief."

Outside, approaching the trading post door, John Kinzie overhears Chiksika talking to Shawnee Chief Blue Jacket. "Ever since the tribal celebration a few days ago things are changing rapidly. I must join my brother on the Wabash. Word is an American army is moving up from Vincennes. Looks like Americans are invading two places."

Blue Jacket responds, "Little Turtle plans to meet in longhouse of Shawnee today and speak about the news he has gathered from Indian spies around the Great Miami River. You not stay for that?"

"Your news may not have anything to do with where I am going. My brother needs me and I must leave immediately to join him and the villages along the lower Wabash."

That midafternoon most of the chiefs of Kekionga, clans and surrounding villages gather inside the Shawnee longhouse for the multi-tribal conference meeting. Running Deer, Hay, Kinzie and Lasselle find a way in during the entrance commotion.

Since she is Little Turtle's sister and has great wisdom, Tah Cum Wah is welcomed with a special seat in the front row of the oblong perimeter.

After all the tribal representatives are inside and seated, Little Turtle slowly stands up to speak.

Respectfully, quietly, the crowd waits for his words.

"Our forefathers, many centuries ago survived a great flood, as you all know, when the great spirit Kitchi Manitou saw disfavor on the earth from great corruption and evilness that had taken over the first populations of this special place in the universe we inhabit. Waters washed away giants and peoples like us, but survivors and animals in a great boat repopulated the earth and spread throughout the lands from then to now."

Little Turtle pauses to take effect. "But evil continues and we war against each other over land continuously. We war to survive.

"Do you remember the stories our ancestors told of defeating the smaller but powerful giants that came back after the flood? How they built the enormous serpent mounds and tall mounds directed by their gods above? They are visible as proof today throughout the world. "The giants devoured our people as food and sacrifice. Our ancestors had no choice but to worship them until they united to stop them. Then, through favorable Manitou, defeated them by hiding and eliminating their food source and overwhelming them while they were in a weakened state."

Blue Jacket stands up. "This is a great history lesson Turtle, but what does this have to do with today?"

"Let him speak, Blue Jacket," Tah Cum Wah demands. "You'll get your chance."

All the hand signing interpretation scattered about the room intermittently comes to a halt until Little Turtle continues.

"We face a great challenge today. As great as the small pox a few decades ago that wiped out this Kekionga land of our people. A challenge as great as the Iroquois, that drove my Miami people many miles into land north and west of here. Greater than even the skillful and courageous Potawatomi hunting in our land," Little Turtle says as he smiles, because he knows the chiefs sitting by from that tribe will be needed in the coming struggle.

"We, all our peoples, have known nothing more than war to survive. Do not we require it of our male youth to go on a war party in order for them to be considered a man? Constant greed, war and takeover of lands have been going on in all civilizations since the beginning of time.

"We pushed the Iroquois back out of our land to the east. Some of our ancestors fought with and against the French and they are now our friends. We had war with and against the English and now they are our friends," he says glancing at Hay in the back. "Evidence of conquering them both lies just a short distance up the Bean River, the intruders call the St. Joseph! The remnants of their forts lie in rubble! They were defeated by the unity and strength we have in our minds and bodies and the Manitou that look after us and give us courage! We survive all intruders! No one can defeat us! And yet," Turtle quietly speaks, barely above the murmur of interpretations and hand signs, "we face the Americans that are building a force of great numbers in Cincinnati, as they call it, on the Ohio.

"They say we have broken the Treaty of Fort Harmar and its predecessor Fort McIntosh. I have signed no such treaty. Have you signed such a treaty?" he asks as he points to the gathering. "Let him stand up and explain this if one is here who signed this so called treaty. Except for Tecumseh, all the great Chiefs in this expansive territory the Americans call the northwest are here in this place, at this time. I know neither Tecumseh nor his brothers have signed it or they would have told me. They are not a fool and neither are we! Some weak chiefs, I have never heard of, have signed it. They do not speak for me! Do they speak for you?"

The longhouse erupts with grunts and moans of negativity. Little Turtle allows the packed house to quiet and then speaks softly with wide eyes, "But, but, we must be smart, cunning and courageous for the whites are coming with many soldiers. Listen to the spies that have come back from watching them."

Little Turtle motions two Miami braves who have just arrived from observing Harmar's army to step forward and give information they have gathered.

After the spies finish, various chiefs stand up to talk either for or against taking on the American army. Some asking if losing the lives of brave warriors is worth it.

Blue Jacket, leader of the Shawnees can hardly contain his desire to conquer and destroy the army preparing to march against him and his nation. Reminding everyone in the room that this is our land and that the British will stand by them, for they are not finished with the Americans themselves.

With beads of sweat forming on his forehead from the heat in the room, Little Turtle arises again and speaks. "Now, take back to your tribes and villages the information you have learned. Trust the information you have received. We meet again in three days. Keep in mind the Americans are but fourteen days march from here."

CHAPTER 6

October 1-14, 1790 - On the Trail from Fort Washington to Kekionga

"Can you believe it, Ben?" E.J. states while packing his gear. "We're about to leave with the first United States military army in its young history, with the best, most experienced general this new country has?"

Ben, with his eyes darting around, answers, "Yeah, have you ever seen so many men and horses together at one time in your life?"

"And Colonel Hardin," continues E.J., "already left three days ago with about 300 militia. This army is going to be even bigger when we catch up with 'em."

"Yep, heard they went up this trail some guy name Clark blazed a few years ago. Guess it's got to be cleaned up or widened so we can get through," recalls Ben.

"Man, look at that will ya? That's the most cattle I've ever seen in one place in my life," says Bobby. "Gotta be over 200 beeves. They going with us, Ike?" asks Bobby getting more comfortable being around E.J.'s uncle.

"I reckon. There is a lot of troops to feed over the next month or so. Cooks'll slaughter 'em as we travel and camp at night."

"All righty, now. Just checkin' on who's goin' in the morning to get a final count," Private John Smith announces to the Pennsylvanians packing. "Some people been desertin' before we even leavin', dang cowards. Ahh, Ben Conrad?"

"Yes sir."

"Don't yes sir me. I'm just a dang private. Although I is in the US army. Yeah, kid, go ahead and call me dat. I kinda like that respect. Besides, I might be gen'ral one day. Ha! Okay, where was I? I'm getting distracted. Elmer James Carlisle?"

"That's me."

Several Penn militia giggle and snort their laughter. "Elmer James? Is that what that E.J. stands for?" Bobby asks grinning.

"Hey, that's a good name. Pro'bly no one else 'round here with it."

"Pro'bly for good reason," smiling Ben says slapping E.J. good naturedly on his buddy's back.

"Before I continue," Smith interjects," if you's got any gun issues, get them checked out today, 'cause it don't look like any new ones comin' in before we leave. Some of you militia here and Kentuckians got a real problem not havin' a musket that fires properly, or even havin' a musket goin' into battle. Hope you's good with a knife and hand to hand if that's the case."

"Better slow down on that whiskey, General," suggests Major David Ziegler inside the headquarters of Fort Washington. "At least till you get those last letters sent out. Your writing is getting a little messy."

"Yes, you're right. Being in the army out here gets to a guy after a while and the whiskey rations allowed can get to a man in other ways."

"Yes, sir. Probably the best decision you made, so far," compliments Zeigler, "was sending Hardin and that large company of Kentuckians outta here ahead of us and away from those scoundrels selling rum to 'em in the town."

"Yeah, free enterprise in action. Ha," Harmar jokingly says. "Speaking of, these land speculators really put the pressure on Congress, Washington and Secretary of War Knox to get things settled out here so they can make money."

"Yes, sir. But the lack of safety is driving a lot of this pressure," converses Ziegler. "These savages are brutally killing innocent people just wanting to make a living."

"Well, dad gum it! Why doesn't Congress give us more money to train more troops to protect them? We had to take the rangers and scouts away from the river to go with both ours and Hamtramck's campaigns," Harmar rants. "There is no one patrolling the river. Dead bodies floating by almost every day. Everybody back east thinks all we have to do is travel up to Kekionga and the Indians will just run scared and leave us alone."

"Maybe they will, sir. Maybe they will sign most any kind of peace treaty just like they did at Marietta and Fort McIntosh in order to keep the peace."

"Major Ziegler, we better hope so. Have you seen the militia that joined us? Why, they're mostly just a bunch of young boys and old geezers. Some fighters are among them but where's Kenton and Boone?" Pausing for another sip of rum, Harmar continues. "We have not had enough time to train these militia up, either."

"Them comin' in late didn't help, sir," adds Ziegler.

"Pressure to get going. My Gosh, we don't even have enough tents for our regulars and did you see the last musket ammo that came in? The cartridges were damaged. It got wet somehow. We won't even know if it works until it is fired!"

"Washington had it pretty bad against the British, sir," says Zeigler, "and we came out okay, General."

"Thanks for your optimism, Major. We can't call it off now. We move out in the morning."

Rat a tat ta tat, rat a tat ta tat, rat a tat tat ta tat... rat a ta tat, rat a tat ta tat, rat a tat tat ta tat...

"All right, look sharp men. We don't want the regulars, marching by here, to think we're slouchers," orders Lieutenant Colonel Truby. "The artillery is next, according to this chart I was given, then the packhorses and cattle. The regulars will form four columns, two columns on each side of the artillery, packhorses and beeves. Then comes us." Looking around at the Pennsylvania militia officers, Truby barks, "We're going to need to form two columns on each side of the camp followers and protect the rear."

"Watch out, Bobby," warns E.J. "Cavalry has to get by with Gen'ral Harmar. Oh, he's gotta nice horse. Sorry you and Ben got knocked down to back up unit. There goes Uncle Ike. He's gotta pretty good lookin' mount, too. They're heading up front to lead the drum and fife corp and flags. Man, this is awesome!"

"You are probably hoping to march next to Charlotte, aren't you, E.J.?" Ben says elbowing E.J.'s arm.

"Hadn't thought of that, but she is going to need protectin'. Right? Ha! Alright, we are movin' now. This is like some parade with all these townspeople sendin' us off."

"I don't know why they call it marchin'. Don't see anybody really in step," Bobby mentions with a puzzled look.

Two miles into the first day's journey, E.J. curiously observes and asks, "What are those guys doin' out there on the side? They are out of the column order. Wonder if Harmar knows they are out there like that?"

"Oh, they are guarding us on the side in case of a surprise attack," offered the long lanky guy wearing the long coat and hat that Fink made fun of. "There are men over on the right, called a flank, too."

"Sorry, sir. Thought I was talkin' to my friend, Bobby. By the way, what you doin' on this mission, mister? You don't look exactly militia and with that long dark coat, hat and carryin' a book. I don't think you're a cook or a blacksmith."

"It's my job to help out in other ways, E.J."

"How'd you know my name?"

"Oh, I get around. And it's the good book I'm carryin."

"Oh, spiritual stuff," E.J. says starting to catch on. I've seen Quaker ministers back in Pennsylvania travelin' around. This is no place for you. That Bible won't be much of a shield from Injun arrows."

"I'm relief to the believers and always hungry to acquire more for Jesus. Harmar and I go back to the Revolutionary War days." Shaking his head slowly and envisioning the past he continues, "It got rough back then."

"Yeah, I was pretty young then but I heard stories," sympathizes E.J.

"I'm not naive to think all people want peace. I'll protect myself if I have to," pulling back his coat to show his flintlock cavalry pistol tucked away in his waist band. "I'm the army Pastor. Look me up if you need some help, E.J."

Averaging about ten miles per day, while stopping to camp at night, the army crosses Hill Creek and Muddy creek, and traverses some rolling slopes. Three days later Harmar's portion of the army meets up with Colonel Hardin and his militia at Turtle Creek and camps to get reorganized.

"Think of it as a big square," explains Major Paul of the Pennsylvania militia. "All the cattle and packhorses go on the inside where the creek is, so they can get watered and fed."

"We better make sure we get our water up stream," interrupts a laughing E.J.

"Umm, you bet, private," continues Paul, "the regulars cover the front line and part of the sides of the square. The militia cover the back half of the sid..."

WHOO AHH AHH, WHOO AHH AHH, WHOO! The sound is repeated.

"Whaas that? asked Ben. We have been on the trail three days and we haven't ever heard that kinda noise."

Others in the ranks stir a bit and a murmur asking the same question finally ends so Major Paul can continue.

"From my experience back home and along the Ohio, the Indians are just letting us know we are being watched," explains Paul. "Get use to it. Injuns gonna try to unnerve ya. Now, as I was sayin..."

The next morning at the front of the Army procession, the brain trust gets ready for the day's march.

"General Harmar," Major Whistler informs as he reads off his official paper, "we have 320 regulars that includes some 120 cavalrymen. The 300 of Hardin's we just joined, added to what we brought along gives us 1133 militia. A couple hundred of which, from what I see, are uncooperative and just along for the pay as substitutes. "Last count, we got 250 camp followers to help out the cookin', military chores and stuff, well, you know, family and such," Whistler concludes, glancing up from his paper at General Harmar.

"Okay," says the General looking back from his saddle atop his horse at the army behind him forming up. "Scout Williams is leading us north on this buffalo trail from here. It is fairly wide at times and narrows occasionally. Lot of Indian villages around, especially near the rivers and streams. Tell all the officers to keep their men attentive. Some natives are friendly, some want our scalps, according to peace negotiators that have been traveling up here the last two years. A couple of whom, by the way, did not come back alive."

"I don't get it, Bobby. Why do you think those regulars gotta wear those tall round hats with feathers sticking up?" E.J. asks striking up a conversation as the army enters into the fifth mile of the fourth day's march.

"I don't know," Bobby says with a concerned expression, "looks like they'd be an easy target. Besides that, the drumming and music we're followin' sure seems to be letting the enemy know we are comin'."

"Maybe that's the idea, intimidate, so they'll be friendly to us," suggests E.J. "Hey, here comes Charlotte!" E.J. exclaims looking over his shoulder.

Running to catch up and catch her breath at the same time, she blurts out, "Hey, Elmer, hello, Bobby," snickering a bit after greeting them.

"Oh, you found out," says E.J. beaming from the attention. "My name sure travels fast. How are things back there, Charlotte? Everybody stayin' up with the pace?"

"I'm doin' good, but as a whole, as you can see, the army is stretchin' out. I bet we are a good quarter mile long. Cattle and pack horses need more prodding cause they are gettin' tired already and we gotta ways to go, don't we?"

"Yeah, according to Major Paul we are a good week or more away from Kekionga. I'm sure the General sees what's goin' on," E.J. adds positively. "Hey, how 'bout I show ya how to fire the musket tonight after sup?"

"Sounds good to me," agrees Charlotte.

At the front of the large force things are a little more serious. Major Whistler rides in from the left flank after consulting with scouts. "General," says Whistler, "Degadaga informs me there is a bear cub all torn apart up ahead."

"So what, Major?"

"It's the redskins' way of warning us not to go farther," Whistler explains.

"Sure some larger animal didn't do that?" asks Harmar.

"Degadaga assures us it is a warning and he has seen Shawnee and Miami spies watchin' us, sir."

"Major, we're not gonna be spooked. Throw the carcass aside so nobody else sees it," orders Harmar.

At camp that night, before dark, E.J. walks Charlotte out away from the campfire. The militia and regulars are passing time in small groups playing dice and card games for money. Some are partaking in their daily whiskey and food rations.

"Whoa you two," advises the posted militia sentry, "don't go out too far, now."

"Don't worry, I just wanna show the lady here how to fire this Charleville," responds E.J.

"Whoa again, we ain't allowin' no firin' of weapons, why the whole camp will go nuts without warnin' them."

"That's okay, E.J.," Charlotte says understandably. "We'll just pretend. I know you gotta keep it loaded so just remind me of the steps Mrs. Thacker showed me back at the fort."

After explaining the loading method, E.J. starts to raise the gun to pretend to shoot when he sees two faces peering out of the bushes nearby, dressed with war paint and three feathers.

"What?" Startled, E.J. accidently squeezes the trigger. Boom! The musket goes off and two Miami Indians scurry away.

"Oh, crap!" exclaims E.J.

The shot causes scrambling of the sentries nearby. "Indians!" yells one of them and points in the direction he thinks they went.

Several militia carrying their muskets and tomahawks break away from camp and give chase. Many from the far side of camp want to know what the commotion is from the shot and quickly come over to the action.

"Ya know I didn't mean to fire, Charlotte," says E.J., as the two walk hurriedly toward camp glancing back over their shoulders.

"The commander will understand, E.J," comforts Charlotte.

"What in tarnation you two strollin' out there that far for?" Lieutenant Colonel Truby, walking out to meet them, sheepishly asks. "Wait, don't answer that. You two have no idea how close you just came to bein' kidnaped or worse! Now I got fellas who've been drinking out there chasin' who knows what. What's worse they may not come back alive."

"Sorry, sir," apologizes, E.J.

"Sir, we have some horses and beeves released and scattered about," says one of the militia sentries from the opposite side of camp that came running when they heard the shot.

"Well, what are the sentries doin' over there? Are they not watching?"

"Ah, ah... no. They came runnin' too, when they heard the shot."

"Oh my goodness, lack of training paying off," Truby states sarcastically and wonders aloud. "What lies ahead?"

"Colonel Hardin! I want a word with Hardin!" orders a disgruntled Harmar the next morning, climbing onto his steed. "I need to know 'bout that gunfire last night and some other things."

"Yes, sir. I'll summon him right away," responds Major Whistler.

"Yeah, you find him and get him up here but we're not wasting daylight. We're movin' out."

The drummers beat away on their drums signaling the call to the troops to line up for the day's march. The flag carriers fall in and the fife players start to play the General's favorite marching music just as Harmar waves his arm forward and gives the verbal order.

Scout Johnny Dee soon gallops in and while riding alongside Harmar updates him speaking over the music, "Degadaga will not be reporting to you personally anymore, General. Not after he got shot at last nite."

"Dad burn, militia. Well I don't blame him. Everybody's jumpy. Young kids learnin' on the march. Noises at night. Indian death signs along the trail. Tell him I understand, and to keep up the good work."

The army proceeds along the buffalo path and through a narrow tree covered passage ordained with tunnel-like branches overhead, when Charlotte walking next to E.J. screams.

"Now what?" asks Major Paul looking back and over the packhorses at the couple.

"Dag nabbit, get that varmint off her," exclaims E.J.

Ben yells to the major, "Just another tree snake, sir!"

"Everytime," complains E.J., "we go through these forest tunnels they drop on somebody or a packhorse or somethin'. Step on that sucker, will you, Ben?" requests E.J.

"Yeah, I got him," says Ben grabbing the reptile by the tail, swinging it around overhead and tossing him into the underbrush.

"Whoa, that's a long one this time," remarks E.J. "You okay, Charlotte?"

Later that morning, Harmar and Hardin catch up with each other.

"I'm tellin' ya, Colonel Hardin, convince your boys to not chase unless they've been given orders. Those two Injuns they scalped and killed last night could have been friendly and given us information. They don't do us any good dead. Besides, those men of yours coulda run right into an ambush."

"Yes, Gen'ral," responds Hardin, "It's just that we ain't used to bein' harnessed to an army. We're used to reactin' and raidin' and revenging. We don't care much for this marchin' to music. We are frontiersmen, fightin' men tryin' to tame these natives here so we can make a livin'. We are sick and tired of our kin and neighbors bein' hauled off who knows where and or kilt by these savages."

"Yes, I understand the emotions that must be going through you and your men on this whole campaign," says Harmar. "Let's try to work together these next couple weeks and show these chiefs out here that American power is not to be doubted."

A few days later, as the army progresses farther north, Indians are continuously being spotted by various military personnel watching the American movement. More cattle and horses are stolen or driven off by the renegades due to the neglect of lazy or tiring troops in charge.

"We're going to start moving northwest, Major Whistler," explains General Harmar, "These creeks and streams around here, the scouts say, are the source of one of the rivers flowing to Kekionga. If we go much farther north we'll get into the Black Swamp area. "The northeasterly movement we've been taking has hopefully kept the Wabash Indians away from us and more near Major Hamtramck's army. This diversion, perhaps, will help us surprise the Miamitown savages."

"I understand, sir. Oh, look at this, Gen'ral," Whistler says, observing Colonel Hardin ride toward them with three militia surrounding an Indian on horseback. "Hardin's men finally obeyed some orders. We got ourselves a captive."

"Good job, Colonel. Major Whistler, halt this army right here. This will help the rear guard catch up a bit and we can question this..., looks like a Shawnee or a Delaware... Get the interpreter! Where's the interpreter?" Harmar orders, looking around from atop his horse, irritated. "Or a signer. Where are people when ya need them? Shoot, the scouts aren't around. Where's Armstrong or Zeigler? Get one or both up here! They know some of this signing or Algonquin language."

Two lieutenants ride off hurriedly looking for the General's ordered request.

A minute later Captain Armstrong rides up to Harmar along with Major Ziegler.

"Captain, Major, what's this Injun got to say?" asks Harmar.

"No guarantee sir, but the Major and I'll try."

"Just ask him what he knows will ya, Captain?" demands Harmar.

Armstrong speaks to the Indian in Algonquin. Not understanding clearly enough, Armstrong resorts to hand signs.

"Sir, I think he says, no, wait, I'm real sure he is indicating Kekionga and villages near there are preparin' to leave," apprises Armstrong. "They think we are too many for them but not sure where we're goin'."

"He not lyin' is he? 'Cause if he's tellin' the truth, we gotta strike real soon," asserts Harmar.

Armstrong holds a sabre up to the Indian while Ziegler asks the same questions. "It's the truth, Gen'ral. He's tellin' the truth," confirms Zeigler.

"I still can't believe Lieutenant Colonel Truby selected me to go with Hardin in the morning to catch those Injuns tryin' to leave Kekionga. That musket goin' off a few days ago was not a good thing," declares E.J. to Ben, Bobby and Uncle Isaac.

"You've learned from that and besides Colonel Hardin needs 600 of the toughest and youngest legs to make the double-time march of 30 miles or so," Uncle Isaac explains.

"Yeah, well, I wish you were going, Ike," states Ben.

"Yes, me too," replies Uncle Isaac, "but the rest of us'll be following 'bout a day behind. You guys'll be okay."

"Hope so, that flatboat skirmish we had on the Ohio gives us an idea what we're up against," a concerned Bobby claims.

Chapter 7

"Before we start to panic," Chief LeGris of the French and Miami village, also known as LeGristown, advises Little Turtle, "we have to be sure they are coming here. We just can't start moving everybody out of Kekionga and burning our homes for no real reason. Where does your information come from?"

"You heard what I heard the other day at the war council, brother-in-law," answers Little Turtle. "Were you not there? Drinking again or hungover? Come on, LeGris, our people need your wisdom."

"You are right, Turtle. That's it. I am done with whiskey and so is my village."

"Now don't be hasty, Chief," says Henry Hay, with his ears perking up while trading a musket to a Piankeshaw Indian for bear furs.

"It would do you good too, Hay," counsels Little Turtle with a smirk. "Listen to me. A war party led by Blue Jacket, will be coming back soon with a firsthand witness account, and maybe a captive or two, of what we got coming at us. Until then, get the word out to start packing."

"Where will we go, Mother?" asks Morning Bird.

"To the northwest. The Eel River Miami and Kickapoo welcome us there as we welcome them here, when there is danger."

"I have never known any other place other than Kekionga. It will be strange leaving here," bemoans Morning Bird.

"We will come back after our braves defeat the white intruders," Morning Bird's mother reassures her.

"Running Deer has been gone with the war party for a number of days now to spy on the great American army. I worry, he won't come back."

"Yes, there is a chance but he is the swiftest, strongest, brightest brave I have seen raised in these villages. He reminds me of Little Turtle."

"Yes, I have heard that comparison," agrees a beaming Morning Bird.

Later that day, Indian war strategy begins in earnest.

"I tell you, they will chase us whenever there is a chance. All we have to do is set the bait," exhorts Blue Jacket to Little Turtle and LeGris. "Let's hear from your captives," demands LeGris. "You just got in here two minutes ago with the white man and the black man and you're all out of breath."

"Ah," Blue Jacket waves his right arm at the prisoners tied together at the stake near the other prisoners. "They are of no value to us. They are not from Harmar's army. We captured them farming on our land near the Little Miami River. Burn them tonight. What do I care if..."

"Wait a minute," Little Turtle interrupts. "Do what you want with the white but the black slave, that's another story. His kind did not invade our world. They come from different place and do not deserve bondage or death from us."

In the Miami village of Kekionga, Running Deer recounts to Morning Bird the war party venture.

"Blue Jacket and I were seconds away from grabbing a white girl and boy from the military invaders. The two had wandered away from camp and walked right toward us when the boy's musket accidently went off after I think he was startled by spotting us hiding in a thicket."

"Wow, Running Deer!" expresses Morning Bird in amazement. "What happened next?"

"We had to scurry away. The soldiers, well, I don't think they were soldiers, but some men carrying muskets not in a uniform, chased after us. But they were easy to hide from. They did grab innocent brothers that lived in a camp near there on down another path."

"What happened to the ones they captured?" asks Morning Bird.

"Ah, it was not good for them, but as Blue Jacket says, he and I live to fight another day when the odds will favor us and we can seek revenge."

"That was a close call, Running Deer."

"Morning Bird?"

"Yes, Running Deer."

"I count three times I was within range to have taken the life of the American Chief Harmar with my musket."

"Why did you not?"

"I probably would not be here to tell you this story. The army on horses, are very fast. The smoke of my musket would have given me away, and the shaft of my arrow if I shot by bow would have pointed at me."

Meanwhile, in Frenchtown, conversation and strategy continues.

"Blue Jacket, let's see what you have in those packhorses that you brought back from the military raid," asks the French trader Lasselle. "Obviously, you didn't just go spying. Ha."

"Speak Shawnee, will you Frenchman?" requests Blue Jacket. "You know I can't understand what you say very well."

"Okay," having to think a little before speaking the Algonquin Shawnee dialect, Lasselle asks Blue Jacket again.

"Go ahead," says Blue Jacket, "but I don't think you'll find anything to trade for."

Peeking into the saddlebags, the Frenchman reacts, "Hmm, I see ammo cartridges for muskets and bayonets. This will come in handy for ya, yes?"

Blue Jacket confirms Lasselle's question and adds, "We decided not to bring back beef cattle. That would have slowed us down. We just scattered about the ones we could. A food shortage later on, perhaps, will help shorten their stay."

"Good thinking, Jacket," praises Little Turtle.

"Tell us about the size of this army," inquires Legris.

"Like I said earlier," advises Blue Jacket, "they are too many for us to conquer as a whole. They have as many with guns, bayonets and spike tomahawks as we have total in our villages, including women and children. We will need many more warriors."

"Are they coming here for sure?" Little Turtle anxiously asks.

"No telling yet, but why would they not? I left a couple of our war party out there to continue to watch. But my friends, this is the capital of our Indian nation. We have many villages and camps around Kekionga. Where else would a large evil snake like that go?"

"Everyone is taking as much food and belongings to the Eel River villages as they can carry," briefs Running Deer's father to his son. "Some things can be buried and then recovered when we come back. But tell me, Running Deer. What is this plan Little Turtle and Legris have come up with that you have overheard? Warriors are staying here to lure white soldiers away from their leader?"

"Yes, father. The Delaware spies assure us that even though they are east of here two days, they are changing directions. Their strategy, it appears, was to throw us off guard and catch us by surprise. Well, we have strategy of our own."

"Okay, I will send your mother and siblings away with the rest of women and children and fight, too. I don't like it, but we must protect our land."

"Look, Kinzie," says Hay, "we gotta get out of here. The wigwams across the river are being hauled off and, oh man..., that's too bad."

"What's that, Hay? asking from the back of the trading post. "What's goin' on"?"

"They are torching the homes over there. The chiefs decided last night at the council that they will leave nothing for the Americans to live in if they stay all winter. They're followin' through with it."

"Yes, I know!" shouts Kinzie from behind a stockpile of goods. "I was there, too. Help me bring these muskets and cartridges out of our building. We gotta give 'em to the Indians. We can't get caught with them. The Americans'll hang us from the highest tree branch if they catch us with "em. In fact, they'll probably hang us if they catch us anywhere near here for any matter.

Procrastination and nervousness prevails in Chief LeGris' village on the banks of the St. Joseph.

"LeGris, your people around here are not moving as they should," Little Turtle warns. "The invaders are less than a day away!"

"I know it!" regrets LeGris, "Some have had too much spirits to drink. They are very hesitant and scared."

"Take this travois I brought over from Kekionga and attach it to this dog," instructs Little Turtle. "This village does not have time to take everything but this will help. They have waited too long to leave. Last I heard the other villages and camps up and down the rivers have been deserted and the warriors from them are meeting us to the north and west near Spy Run Creek."

"Okay, yes, yes. Thank you." responds LeGris.

"Must I remind you of your own idea to cover the back side of our evacuation?" says Little Turtle. "The defensive plan will then go into motion."

Chapter 8

October 15-18, 1790 - Kekionga

"I knew when we camped last night we were getting close," exclaims E.J. breathing heavily, running down a slight grade next to Ben Conrad, Bobby Fulton and other militiamen. "I think I see scouts Williams and Johnny Dee stopped up ahead."

"Where's Colonel Hardin's cavalry, though," utters a breathless Bobby looking through slight haze and smoke.

"Dang, they could be fightin' Injuns right now," replies Ben pulling his packhorse reins with one hand and carrying his musket with the other. "Be ready to shoot."

Major Ziegler, in charge of the foot soldiers, is seen walking to the left at the edge of the river bank overlooking Kekionga, toward the American scouts.

E.J. holds up his hand and slows down muttering, "Take it easy. If there was trouble he'd be waving and pointin' at us in different directions."

"Good thinkin', E.J." compliments Bobby. "Let's spread out and see for ourselves what they're lookin' at."

Discontinuing the hurried pace, walking up to and peering down from the river rim, Ben declares, "No wonder these Injuns like this place."

"Yeah, well," Bobby adds, "too bad we didn't get here before they set their villages on fire and all the smoke is in the air."

"I agree," says E.J. "There's the two rivers comin' in from the left formin' what Hardin calls the Omee," E.J. points out from his vantage point, "but I think it's really called the Miami or Maumee. Actually, I don't care what they call it. Our cavalry is down there checking out this village and is vulnerable to an attack."

"Yes, at least our scouts are on the edge of the cornfields. Man, that is a lot of corn. Lotta Indians must live here or did live here and may be watchin'," Bobby says cautiously gazing left to right and then glancing behind him.

Scrutinizing from the forested hardwood trees to the north and west, Running Deer and fifty other Indian warriors observe the Americans browsing through the smoldering cabins, houses and other debris in Kekionga. With tears streaming down his war painted face he remembers his boyhood of swimming, fishing and game playing.

Running Deer shakes his head slowly. "They will pay for this. Won't they Little Turtle?"

With steely eyes, Little Turtle responds, "our Manitou will guide us to know when. For now, be strong."

Chief Legris, squatting next to Little Turtle, advises, "Let them get more confident and bolder. They will chase and be easy to defeat later on."

"I would attack now. My blood is boiling for fight. I have no patience or stomach for this," interjects Blue Jacket.

"I admire your courage, my friend," commends Little Turtle, "but even my son-in-law Black Snake patiently awaits revenge on his former people."

William Wells silently nods his head in agreement with the Miami chief.

Little Turtle continues, "We need the Potawatomi, Kickapoo, Ottawa and others to show up to fight with us. There are too many Americans in our village and more coming down the embankment crossing the Omee. We have them surrounded now but too few warriors to conquer them. Let's see how careless their spies get looking for us and how overconfidently their leaders try to track us down."

A day later, General Harmar follows the drum and fife musicians across the Maumee ford that leads to Kekionga. The main force of the army and camp followers trail him. Approaching Harmar from Kekionga on horseback to greet the General is a saluting Major Ziegler.

"What in the world is goin' on, Ziggy?" asks Harmar.

"Well, sir. Things are a little outta hand."

"A little out outta hand? I thought it was possible there would be some booty to be had but, criminy, this isn't some gold rush. Where's Hardin? Get me Colonel Hardin for goodness sake! This is his mess!"

Attempting to settle Harmar down, "let's ride across this ford here, General, and get a better look at what we got in this village," offers Major Whistler, the General's officer of the day and accompanied by Lieutenant Ebenezer Denny. "Let our horses and cattle drink a little water too, and then we'll go up the bank up ahead. It's about time for lunch, also."

"All right," General Harmar agrees gazing around, "let's get the 'dad gum' camp organized." Looking back across the river he yells, "Wave the rest over, Lieutenant Denny! I don't know what the heck they're waitin' on. The river isn't but a foot deep in this area.

"Is that Private Smith over there on the St. Joseph, rope-swingin' into that river hole actin' like a kid? That's a bunch of youngsters with him. Denny, get'em clothed. Skinny dippin's gotta stop. Women and children camp followers are comin' across soon."

Colonel Hardin rides his mount into the river splashing toward Harmar and the other officers that are gathered. Shaking his head, "I know what you're gonna say, General. I don't like all the lootin' either. Here's the report though; we count at least six vacant Indian communities up and down the rivers full of kettles and a few other items the redskins left behind. But the big village, we are in front of, has done the most damage to itself. The other five are bein' rummaged as we speak."

"Colonel, is there no regard for safety?" asks Harmar. "How can you be sure the savages are gone? From the looks of what has been left behind, they evacuated in a hurry and can't be that far away. And did you say six villages?"

"Yes, sir, at the minimum, six," Hardin answers. "Two up the St. Mary's, two on either side of the St. Joseph here, one on up the St. Joseph and one down the Maumee, called Chillicothe. All are within' two or three miles of where we are right now."

"That's a lot of riled redskins out there. Where's the scouts? Where's Daniel Williams? Find him, Captain Armstrong, and bring him here. We gotta know what's out there beyond these rivers and corn fields!"

"Yes, sir, right away, sir," Armstrong says galloping away.

"Major Ziegler," demands General Harmar, "make yourself useful and gather the officers in for a meeting in one hour. We'll eat then."

"Yes, sir."

"One thing we might want to have the cook's fix, Major Whistler, is corn. Ha. Plenty of it here. The rests gotta be destroyed and burned along with all the shelters and whatever these scoundrels use before we leave for home. If we can't beat'em on the battlefield we can starve 'em to death this coming winter."

"Pardin me Gen'ral," interrupts Colonel Hardin, "but it's like our troops have some kinda fever. Some silver was found along with food under a replanted bush, and ever since then the troops been diggin' like crazy."

"The regulars that were in your command are gonna stop that real soon and join those comin' across the river. We have to set up a defense. Have you encountered any Indians, Colonel?"

"Yes, sir. The cavalry, yesterday, chased down two that wandered into their village on the other side of the St. Joseph. Scalped 'em and oh, no..."

"Any information, Colonel?" asks Harmar, "before you... I thought we learned that lesson! What about those bloody British and French traders that lived here? Any of them found?"

"Trading posts have been located and pillaged of what's left, Gen'ral, and are burning," apprises Hardin. "The traders themselves, we think, have skedaddled. To where, we don't know."

The next morning E.J. walks toward a gathering force of regular federals and militia for an army expedition.

Stretching his arms, he glances over at one of his friends and comments. "Ben, I'm glad the rest of the army and Harmar is in camp now. I feel a little safer. And after all that swimmin' yesterday, I gotta good night's rest. That Smith is hilarious."

"Ha," laughs Ben. "Yep, it felt good to get clean, too. But, seriously though, what do we know 'bout this Colonel Trotter that's leadin' us on this three day excursion?"

"I heard he's a friendly guy," answers E.J. "Kentuckians seem to like him better than Hardin."

"That's good to hear," replies Ben. "Feelin's from some are that the Indians would have attacked by now if they were around."

Uncle Isaac rides his grey mare up alongside the strolling boys.

"Hey, Unk, good to see you," greets E.J. "Looked for ya yesterday. It sure is a big camp. There's gotta be hundred campfires around here."

Gazing down from his horse, "the feelings mutual, nephew. Hi, Ben. I see Bobby comin' over. You guys doin' okay?"

"Yeah, we're doin' alright, Ike," answers Ben confidently.

"Hey," offers Ike, "this new leader Trotter has been given a chance to command a force to the northwest following lotsa tracks that go that way. Be at the ready. Okay, fellas? Harmar's sending 300 of us. I hope it's enough... oops, the cavalry's formin' up to move out. I gotta go. I'll see ya later."

"Okay," E.J. says giving a wave to his uncle. "He seems a little nervous, fellas."

Bobby asserts, "Prob'bly a good reason. I heard some horses and cattle got taken last night. Sentries suppose to be watchin' 'em, fell asleep. They got yelled at a while ago. No whiskey rations for them tonight. Besides that, the older veterans figure the Injuns are waitin' for us to make a mistake."

Forty cavalrymen and scouts lead the way riding up front with Lieutenant Colonel Trotter. The rest of the brigade of thirty regulars, and 230 riflemen with fixed bayonets march the track grooved trail leading away from Kekionga. Consisting of three columns of foot soldiers, the regulars occupy the middle column and the militia are single file on each side.

After traveling a couple miles, everything appears normal with the men marching alertly. The silence is broken only by the cavalry horse hooves pounding the beaten path that's tunneled by hardwood trees on either side. Some leaves changing into their autumn colors add beauty to the scenery but belies the danger ahead. The quiet pace is interrupted by strange bird-like sounds. Then stunningly, partially wrapped deceased Indian bodies platformed up near the forest canopy are noticed by the troops. As the columns slow, all heads passing by underneath are tilted up and to the left, eyes gazing into the trees.

"Nothin' to worry bout. Seen it before," Private Smith breaking the silence states. "The natives have a strange way of buryin' their dade. They'll haul'em down an put 'em in the ground in a few days. Somethin' bout their spirit has to rise first. The only spirit I like to rise is in my cup. Ha."

Anxious laughter by those who had heard Smith relax the men somewhat, but not for long.

"What the heck?" Bobby expresses, eyes looking up the trail at the front of the company. "Two horsemen just took off to the left and there goes a third one, lickety split."

"Yeah, I saw that, Bobby," says Ben. "The columns are startin' to hold up."

Bam, Bam, bam....

Guns go off at the front of the detachment and horsemen bust out of the musket smoke, this time, racing to the right.

"Get off the path and take cover," shouts Major Hall, Trotter's subordinate waving his arm to direct the militia on the right to move into the brush to the right.

"Get down, stay down! Watch behind ya and spread out on the wings," says Hall ordering the militia and regulars on the left and middle to move to the left. "Injuns might come running to the gun fire."

E.J. whispers to his buddies, "I think I saw some officers go ridin' off when those shots were fired. Can't miss those hats they're wearin'. They'll be right back, I hope."

A long thirty minutes go by when the cavalry rides back to the force holding the head of a dead Indian.

"Here come some more back in," Ben notices giving an account of what he's seeing. "Just a scalp this time. One of ours is wounded. They're gonna ride the injured cavalryman by us, probably back to camp. His arm... he's holding his arm. Looks like he's gonna fall off his horse," says Ben, while all eyes are following the wounded and two cavalrymen riding on each side of him, assisting.

"It wasn't Ike, was it?" asks E.J.

"Don't think so," replies Ben.

"All right, everybody back on the trail," orders Hall. "We are movin' out."

Observing from thickets on a hill merely eighty yards away, Little Turtle utters. "They got one of our braves but he put up a great, honorable fight."

"He got too close to lure more of them away and into our trap. His horse was not fast enough to escape," reasons Legris.

"Who was the other the invaders got?" asks Running Deer. "I did not recognize him."

No one responds to the young warrior.

"Let's replan this," directs Little Turtle. "Up ahead on the trail the Americans follow, will be a better spot to ambush them. Let's get them farther from Kekionga so no help can reach them. Maybe they will branch off some more."

"Blue Jacket is going to please his Manitou," LeGris mentions while a grin then turns to a frown. "Unfortunately, our sorrow goes out to our dead warrior and his family. We can never afford a loss. Warrior numbers are getting smaller..."

BOOM!

"What was that thunder on a clear day?" asks Running Deer.

"American cannon," responds Chief LeGris, "it is used to project a big heavy ball to knock down walls of forts."

"Why did they fire that off?" inquires Running Deer.

"Don't know," answers Little Turtle. "The fort the British and French built on the St. Joseph is already in ruins. No need for... what are these Americans doing? They have stopped."

"They're turning around," the astonished LeGris says observing.

Back at the camp in Kekionga, Majors Whistler and Zeigler sitting near the main campfire, look up from their late afternoon cider and notice Colonel Trotter riding slowly toward them with his 300 man detachment following.

Walking briskly toward Trotter, Whistler swallows what's left in his cup and in bewilderment asks, "What are you doing back already? Did you suffer more casualties? Get the surgeon ready, Ziegler! What happened, Trotter? Are Injuns following you?"

"Ahh, ah, no," stammers Trotter. "We heard the cannon go off and I thought the Gen'ral was signaling us to come back in."

Colonel Hardin walking up hears the explanation. "Lieutenant Colonel Trotter, you were given provisions for three days and, how could you mistake direct orders to journey for three days. The cannon was for the troop detachments scattered about the Indian villages here to return. How did you hear the cannon? You should have been several miles out."

Chapter 9

October 19, 1790 - Kekionga

At sunrise Major Ziegler knocks on the support pole outside General Harmar's tent.

"General Harmar?"

"Yes, come in."

Observing the General holding a lit candle in one hand and a razor in the other while staring into a small mirror, shaving, he salutes and states, "Ah, you may want to see this."

"What now, Major? It's bad enough Trotter came back early yesterday. Are Hardin and his men getting ready to depart?"

"As far as I know they are. But this happened overnight, sir," opening the tent flap.

"Who is that?" Harmar inquires viewing a blood stained head of an Indian mounted on a pole sunk into the loose soil a few feet away from his tent. "Who did this and how did that get here without guards allowing it?"

"It appears to be a mystery, sir," Ziegler retorts. "No one admits to seeing anything happen last night."

"That face looks familiar. It is not Miami, Shawnee or from around here. Crap, we are now short one scout, Major. That's, ah, Degadaga."

Five miles north and west of Kekionga a confederation of warriors awake around their campfire eating cornbread and stew.

"We must take some action. Are the whites leaving for their fort soon or are they coming here to find our families?" ponders Blue Jacket aloud.

"The Americans are not stupid. They can see the tracks our people made coming this way to the Blue Lake and Eel River camps to escape them," responds Little Turtle.

Chief LeGris joins the discussion and interjects. "I question their decision to send small forces to find us. We can defeat that tactic. Our spies should be coming soon to tell us what is going on with the whites. But maybe they are satisfied with the destruction of our villages and will leave us."

Little Turtle walks up and gives an update, "Many of the braves we called for from other tribes to help us are thinking it is not worth dying against such a large enemy. Some, to our southwest, have gone to help Tecumseh and his brothers against this white chief Hamtramck coming up the Wabash River. Some farther down the Maumee worry about Harmar coming to their villages. Cannot blame them, the white Chief still might."

Blue Jacket stands up to emphasize his suggestions, "I say we act today even if they do not come this way and before they leave to the south or anywhere. From what I have seen with my own eyes they are foolish, overconfident and question our bravery. They must be taught a lesson to never come back here again! There is no place in our land for these long knives to live among us!"

"I agree, but we must be smart, Blue Jacket. I like your aggressive desires but do you not understand this?" asks LeGris.

As Charlotte walks E.J. toward the military detachment lining up to be sent out with Colonel John Hardin this time, she speaks up. "When you get back in two days or so you are welcome to eat with my family. The catfish and rock bass from the river are mighty tasty."

"Thanks for the invite, Charlotte, and I'll surely take you up on that but the meal may not be held here. Word is, the camp is moving on down the river to Chillicothe to finish destroying that village."

"Yes, that makes sense," says Charlotte. "There's not much more destruction that can be done in this Indian settlement. Besides, the smoke from all the burning is getting nauseous. My mother and others have been encouraging the officers to head back to Fort Washington. How much more can the army destroy? The Injuns are gone. There's no one to fight."

"Well, we'll know more after today. We're heading back nor'west, followin' the tracks we saw yesterday only farther."

"Hmmm, doesn't look like as many are goin' with ya today, E.J.," remarks Charlotte.

"What's goin on, Bobby?" asks E.J. walking up to him and looking around. "Where is everybody? Should be the same as yesterday, at least, don't ya think?"

"Some don't wanna go with Hardin," reasons Bobby. "Some don't wanna go 'cause of the head they saw before it got buried. They are scared. Some ready to go back home. Family is pressurin' 'em."

"We have a whole camp full of soldiers. Surely we will get some replacements," E.J. says hopefully.

"Yep. I heard Major Paul and Colonel Truby are workin' on it. Bringin' in some more Pennsylvanians, too." Bobby says with some enthusiasm.

"Alright, Charlotte, we are going to be okay. Captain Faulkner is leadin' our column today and... Ha. There's Smith up there with the commander of the regulars Captain Armstrong and Ensign Hartshorn ahead of the militia leading the right column."

"Look at that Ike goin' up front of the cavalry," Ben observes approaching his friends with his bayonet fixed musket pointed up on his shoulder. "Ooh wee, look at him, right next to the Major Fontaine. He is a big shot. Ha."

"See, Charlotte? We'll be okay. No need to worry."

"E.J.?"

"Yes, Charlotte?"

Drawing E.J. close to her and giving him a hug. "Be careful... okay?"

Later that morning just past where Trotter's detachment turned around, scout Daniel Williams rides in on the forest lined trail from the northwest to report to the task force leader Colonel Hardin.

The night before, after some extensive pleading by Hardin, he received the assignment from General Harmar.

"They're out there, sir," reports Williams. "Lot's of signs. Where they are exactly I do not know. We miss Degadaga. He was scouting the southwest until yesterday when he moved into this area. He was smart. It was not like him to get taken out like he was."

Hardin nods in agreement, "yes, I understand. He seemed to know the Northwest Territory well."

Williams snaps back to reality and advises, "there is a fresh camp up ahead a mile. I would say fifty or more were there last night. Fresh tracks go farther up the trail, but it could be some sort of trick. Injuns might be coming back."

"Good observation, Danny. Let's move up, spread out and form a semi-circle trap around that camp, two men deep and back far enough we don't shoot each other with cross fire." Hardin looks around and spots who he wants.

"Major Fontaine?"

"Yes, sir," answers the cavalry commander.

"Did you hear Williams?" asks Hardin.

"Yes, sir."

"Okay, you keep the cavalry back behind the troops for now so the horses don't give us away. You hear gun shots, you come a ridin' up the trail, you hear! And I'll be directin' ya."

After setting the trap an hour goes by and Hardin reconsiders the strategy. Thinking that this is a waste of time, he orders the cavalry forward on up the trail followed by Armstrong's regulars and Hartshorn's Kentucky columns.

Thirty minutes go by when scout Johnny Dee rides up from behind, past the reluctant but moving army and alongside Hardin.

"Pardon me, Colonel, did you mean to leave the Pennsylvanians back there at that Indian camp you had entrapped?"

"Yeah, well, no, Johnny," responds Hardin. "We've been followin' these hot tracks, dang it." Glancing around for someone to blame, "What happened, Armstrong?" spotting him in front of his column.

Not waiting for Armstrong to answer, Dee continues, "Besides that, Colonel, I saw some of your militia headin' back to Kekionga quite a while ago. You probably only got about 180 troops with ya all together. But even them are gettin' strung out. They can't or won't stay up with ya."

"Dang, all right, let's hold up a bit here." Eyeing Major Fontaine riding in, Hardin greets him. "Good to see you comin' back. What's up ahead? Whata ya got?"

Pulling up in front of Hardin, the cavalry leader answers him, "The scouts and I just got done chasin' some Injuns but they got away disappearin' into the forest like it was nothin'." Catching his breath, Fontaine finishes. "There's definitely fresh tracks leadin' northwest, Colonel."

"Okay. Good job. I gotta special request for ya, Maja'. I need you to ride with some cavalry back down the trail to Captain Faulkner. He's still at the Injun camp. Order him forward, pronto. We are not waitin' here, though. In my opinion it would be a good thing for us to eliminate some of these renegades before we head back to Kekionga tomorrow."

"Yes sir, can't argue with ya on that, Colonel. That's what we is out here for."

Fontaine gathers ten cavalrymen and at full gallop heads down the trail past Captain Armstrong and Hartshorn's strung out columns.

Armstrong steps alongside Hardin and looks up, "Colonel, we have but thirty infantry with us here. We are vulnerable for an attack. There could be hundreds of warriors around us. The Indians have had plenty of time to organize and bring in help from other villages."

"Okay, okay, bring Hartshorn's column of militia on the double alongside of ya, Captain," Hardin anxiously responds. "Let's move forward. The day's gettin' shorter. I think I see somethin' unusual ahead."

Up the trail, Little Turtle and Blue Jacket lay obvious tracks leading to a low somewhat marshy and swampy area of a small open prairie surrounded with sporadic underbrush, spruce, elm and hardwood trees.

"Running Deer, direct the warriors in building three campfires," requests Chief LeGris. "Little Turtle, you know the trap and the signals as do all the braves. It is good that more friendly brothers, even though a few, from other tribes have joined us. They now see the danger we face, first hand."

"I agree. They bolster our numbers, obviously, but don't go wandering off. Okay, LeGris? I know the pressure is great but we need you here."

"Our messenger spies approach with smiles," notices the curious Blue Jacket as the riders come closer. "Let me see. What is draped over the captured horse? Hmmm, dead American scout, maybe? What do you think, LeGris?"

"Prop him up against a tree next to the fires for further enticement," LeGris answers signing and speaking Algonquin to communicate to the different tribesmen gathered. "Now then, we need to split up. Forty to each side of Little Turtle behind the fires. I have war paint if you need some."

A few minutes later Little Turtle confidently exhorts and reassures the warriors.

"We must take a stand, here. The intruders must go no farther! This is it! They will be here soon for us to destroy! This is our land the intruders have plundered, razed and burned! In a short time these invaders will be ours. Be strong!"

With the emotions of the warriors almost uncontainable, Little Turtle knows when to temper and then instruct the grimaced faced warriors.

"Now we go silent with hand signals, but you Miami, listen for bird sound instructions as well. Blue Jacket, you and Blacksnake place yourselves midway on each flank to relay battle orders."

As Little Turtle, in back of the main fire, hidden by a tree extends his arms out and flickers his fingers, the forty warriors on each side of him understand they must extend in a straight line farther, crouching low to the ground. Carrying their muskets with attached bayonets or, if they do not have a gun, a bow, quiver and tomahawk, intermittently, they glance back at Little Turtle for the next hand signals.

Nature all around them resumes its natural buzz and chatter for a mid-October afternoon as if nothing is going to happen.

Colonel Hardin presses forward toward the decoy fires. Slowly now, through the open marshy meadow and swamp, the horses trudge with their riders atop, followed by Armstrong's regulars and Hartshorn's militia that are strung out behind.

"Hey, it's one of our scouts," Colonel Hardin expresses viewing ahead fifty yards. "As good a place to camp as any, I reckon, but we still have daylight to travel."

Holding up his arm to signal his procession to stop, Hardin turns to Armstrong, "Somethin's fishy, let's halt here."

After a brief pause that allows more troops forward, Armstrong insightfully notices and murmurs to Hardin, "I agree, Colonel, that scout is motionless. We may have an issue up ahead or right here."

With a flick of Little Turtle's hand and fingers the warriors on the left and right wing tips crawl low to the ground bending a large semi-circle encasing the military forces gathering. Within seconds, when all the troops that are with Hardin are within the Indian range, Little Turtle flicks the left hand fingers only. The signal draws the warriors up out of their crouch with muskets aimed and the drawing of arrows back. Blue Jacket ignites his musket first followed by the rest.

Down go militia, regulars and horses alike, instantly killed or wounded. The American survivors, that are able, move instinctively to their left. A flick of Little Turtle's other hand and fingers this time, springs up the Indian right flank and a deadening wall of musket balls are projected into the stunned troops causing more death, panic and the running and riding of some militia back down the trail they had, a few minutes prior, traipsed forward on.

"Hold your ground, men!" orders Armstrong to the regulars and militia, "Form a defense! Form a line! Fire into the underbrush when ready and reload!"

Little Turtle, anticipating this, drops his braves to the ground with the motion of both hands. After most of the American's returning lead balls miss their targets or fly over the enemy's head, the command to attack is made. "AAYIAAYI!," yells Little Turtle while waving forward his right arm."

"AYYYAY YAYA!" is chorused by the attacking warriors.

After a sprint of a few yards toward the Americans, hand to hand combat, thrusting bayonets missing and making deadly contact alike, brings screaming agony of pain or the exuberating finishing off of an enemy.

Hardin rides back down the trail to rally the numerous terrified militia. "Stop! There is no retreatin'! Turn around! Return the fire! Pick up your weapons!"

"Are you crazy, Colonel?" one militiaman gasps while fleeing, "Get the heck outta here!"

Observing the Americans that stayed to fight, Hardin rides back to the smoke infested melee of former colonists and Native Americans. Brandishing his sabre, the Kentucky Colonel makes contact against thrusting bayonets to block, and searches for human bodies to destroy.

Blood flying everywhere, one by one the regulars and militia fall to the fury of warriors defending their home land.

Armstrong, somehow remaining unscathed, discerns the fruitlessness of not having the numbers to win the field reluctantly but smartly shouts, "Retreat! Retreat!"

"Ayyyeeee!! Pursue! Pursue!" screams Blue Jacket.

"Ayyyee!" howls, Running Deer, fearlessly chasing down, scalping and disposing three retreating soldiers himself.

"You hear somethin', E.J.?" asks Ben as the Pennsylvanians, led by Captain Faulkner, fast walk up the trail following Fontaine and ten cavalry that were sent back by Hardin to bring up the eighty refocused company of militia.

"Yeah, and it's getting' louder," answers E.J.

"You see something, Uncle Isaac?" asks E.J.

"Yep, we've got a stampede of some sort comin' through the forest and down the trail... right at us!"

"Hundreds of Injuns, comin' after us! Run for your lives!" yells a delirious, open mouthed militiaman darting past the Pennsylvanians with blood streaming down from his missing ear.

"Movin' forward!" orders Fontaine swinging his arm to signal an advance. "Let's see what's goin on!"

More militia with blood stained clothes, and others weaponless without injury, race past.

"There are more of ours comin' down the trail with Injuns chasing! Form a defense here," Fontaine says, waving his arms left and right. "Across the trail and into the woods, let's move! Behind logs, whatever! And I do not want to see anyone joining the panic! I'll shoot ya myself!"

"Be ready to fire!" orders the militia leader, Faulkner. "Be sure it's an Injun!"

Believing they were invincible, the warriors charge straight at the awaiting militia.

"Fire, men!" commands Faulkner and Fontaine almost simultaneously.

E.J., Ben, Bobby and Uncle Isaac, who had dismounted and joined the trio, squeeze off their rounds holding the barrel still until the mini ball finally leaves their musket through the smoke of gunpowder. The surviving braves and those following are caught by surprise and turn around stooping to avoid further gunfire and to gather their fallen brothers.

Not knowing the circumstances ahead, the Pennsylvanians are ordered to reload and slowly backup covering the backside of the retreat.

Chapter 10

BOOM!

Another loud cannon shot is fired and echoes off trees lining both sides of the river. This time the shot is to let the stragglers, coming back from the battle up by Eel River know that the military encampment was now in Chillicothe, two miles downstream from Kekionga.

"A time to tear and a time to mend, a time to be silent and a time to speak, a time to love, and a time to hate, a time for war, and a time for peace," finishes the Pastor after reading Ecclesiastes 3:1-8 in the Bible.

Hugging to comfort the sobbing wives and children, in camp, of those known killed in the bloody skirmish proved difficult whether they were a believer or non-believer in God. The shock of the defeat had a long way to go before wearing off, if ever. Militia and regulars from the late afternoon battle started coming in soon after supper. Some family and friends were still waiting hopefully for a loved one, to somehow, miraculously, return even at this early hour of a new day.

Scattered about, soldiers from the excursion gathered to unwind around the campfires.

"I still can't sleep. I've got to be one of the luckiest son of a guns," exclaimed Private John Smith. "Did I tell ya the redskin was fallin' down on me with his tomahawk ready to finish me off when I..."

"Yes..." replied E.J. "You raised your bayoneted musket jus' in time and the Injun done fell on it."

"Guess I had..." Smith says, shaking his head.

"Then struggling to get the dead Injun's bleedin' weight off of ya, you were able to crawl away just as the redskins started chasin' the retreatin's," finished Bobby.

"I'd say the Lord's given ya another chance, Smitty," submits the Pastor wandering by, overhearing the story for the first time.

"Here, Mr. Smith, have some more cider. It might settle you down," offered Ben.

Uncle Isaac tries to offer some comfort, "Smith, I would have been up there with you if Fontaine hadn't pulled me and some other cavalry back to bring E.J. and these guys forward. Maybe ten more of us with ya might have turned the tide."

Bam, bam, bam... bam, bam, bam.

Guns go off in the distance startling the camp patrons and recuperating combatants alike.

"Now what?" asks Uncle Isaac getting up from the fire and walking to get his horse. "I'll check on it. Grab your Charleville's. Have you reloaded since we've been back? We don't seem to be done with them savages, yet."

Back at the previous afternoon's battle site near the Eel River, the Miami, Shawnee and other tribesmen dance in victory around a fire near the dead Americans scattered about. The follow up butchery chasing the fleeing militia down the trail and in the forest was simply more gratifying.

"The whites are done. They will not want more of this," boasts Running Deer during the pole calumet. "The scalps around my waist proves my manhood to defend my home land!"

As the campfire licks from added logs the braves stand up and dance to the beat of the Indian drums. Some, waving still dripping blood stained scalps they had taken, show no sign of needing rest.

"Come on, Hartshorn," whispers Captain Armstrong, near the celebratory dance, crawling out of a swamp pond he had escaped into during the retreat.

"Geeez, you just scared me to death," Hartshorn answers, slithering out from under a fallen rotting tree trunk. "How'd you know I was there?"

"Shhhh, follow me."

After the Indians dance awhile another tomahawk slams into the pole that was upright next to the campfire.

"The whites are not warriors like us. They caccannot deefeat us," exclaims Chief LeGris slurring his speech and signing at the same time. "They run at the ssight of our courage, cunningness and bbravery. They are on their way back to their ffather chief Washington as we celebrate. AHHAWWA!"

Several warriors sitting, listening and cheering are frightened by the movement toward them out of the darkness.

"Morning Bird... you made it here," Running Deer declares very pleased as she comes to sit next to him. "I think the invaders are long gone. Is everything okay in our new village up the river?"

"Yes, everything is okay. Many of us squaws could not sit around any longer after we heard the good news of the victory and came as soon as we could. We brought the healing power of the shaman for the injured, also."

"We lost some brave warriors, Morning Bird. Much sorrow goes out to the clans and immediate family who lost loved ones. We mourn with them."

Morning Bird pointing toward the three American prisoners tied up nearby with their knees drawn up to their faces as if to hide, asks, "You get any information from them?"

"Oh yes, Harmar has a big army but few fighters. It will still take more warriors though to conquer them. These three are not adoptable. They were running like scared pheasants. They will not last the night."

At the same time the Indians danced, inside General Harmar's tent at Chillicothe, the mood is different.

"Those gunshots, I hope, are a good sign that we got the horse thieving renegades," General Harmar, gulping another whiskey says to Majors Whistler and Zeigler. "Check on that will ya, Whistler?"

"Yes, sir, and if the troops that are setting the trap, have captured any savages, I'll bring them in for questioning."

"Now we are thinking 'round here, Major Whistler! You may even command a fort someday." Pacing the tent floor, Harmar thinks aloud and rambles. "That dang Hardin. Never shoulda let him take that unit out there yesterday. I thought with his experience goin' on Indian raids before, he could handle that expedition. But, no. He leads his force into an ambush.

"And Ziegler, what do we do with the cowards, the deserters? Course, some of them are halfway back to Kentucky or Pennsylvania by now. Should we line 'em up and shoot 'em tomorrow? We can't have that type of behavior! Dang, I knew this army was not ready to go on this campaign," continues Harmar.

"Hmmm, Indians don't usually attack at night but they may try some tricks. Isn't that right, Major Ziegler?"

"Huh? Wa zat, sir?"

"Wake up, Major! We could be under attack. We need to finish up burning and destroying this Shawnee village tomorrow, I mean today. A few wigwams and cabins on the other side of the river, too. I think they're Delaware over there and Shawnee here. We gotta prepare to head back too. Don't we, Zeigler?"

A bright full moon during the night leads to a cloudless daybreak as the coalition of warriors begin to awaken.

The stench of death permeates the dawn air.

"Our dead have been taken care of, but these whites we do not touch," Little Turtle states. "The birds and animals will take care of them. Our wounded go to our new home with the squaws and shaman. What about you, Black Snake? Is your damaged arm a hindrance?"

"Shaman has a medicine for this," William Wells says holding up the injured limb.

"You were very brave during the battle," praises Little Turtle. "It cannot be easy fighting your own blood."

"I am not of the white blood anymore, father-in-law. Do not my actions and Algonquin language convince you? So don't even suggest that. My question to you and LeGris is, do I enter the American army as a white man and spy what their next movements will be?"

"Good question, Black Snake. Where is LeGris, by the way?" asks Little Turtle peering around. "We will be leaving soon to go to Kekionga, and get a sense of what's going on, and perhaps what we can salvage. Let us discuss that on our way. If the Americans are leaving, as we hope, that may not be a necessary chance you will need to take."

Outside of General Harmar's tent that morning, many camp followers and family of soldiers want answers to their request for the army to leave for Fort Washington.

"We are not leaving yet," says Major Whistler, attempting to calm the crowd down. "You people knew what you were getting into when you decided to come along. The army appreciates all you have done for it on this campaign. But some of you complaining have done nothing but complain the entire expedition, so go back to your campsite and wait for orders unless you want to venture back to Cincinnati yourself."

Inside the tent, Harmar, Hardin and the extremely lucky Armstrong finish reviewing what happened at the previous day's battle.

"We need to go back up there and bury our dead," insists Armstrong. "That's the least we can do, General."

Harmar shaking his head, "I tell you, it is not reasonable. Chances are there are at least a thousand warriors gathered by now ready to finish us off. You hear those people outside this tent? Do they sound like they want to go farther north and see the results of what may happen to them? No, Captain. It is not gonna happen."

Harmar then turns his attention to address the expedition leader, Colonel John Hardin. "Colonel, we lost twenty-two regulars out of thirty that were with you. Nine militia fought and died bravely. A hundred left the battlefield and we don't know where they went or if they are alive. Are they afraid to come back to camp? Are they on their way back home? I will take responsibility for not taking the time to train them up. But let's be honest, Colonel, we have mostly inexperienced kids and older guys. The regulars, by the way Captain Armstrong, from all reports were outstanding yesterday."

The new day in Chillicothe, after the battle near Eel River, brings a clearer vision of the results and contemplation by E.J. and his companions.

"The camp has gotten a lot quieter, hasn't it, Ben?" asks E.J.

"Yeah, since ya mention it. Maybe reality is settin' in. Everybody's finishin' breakfast an' headin' out to tend to the burnin' and stuff. I hope those sentries are watchin' real close out there."

"Fellas?"

"Yeah, Bobby?" responds E.J.

"That coulda been us up front with Hardin yesterday," says Bobby finishing his cornmeal mush. "Why, some of those guys didn't have a chance."

"Hey fellas," greets the Pastor walking by. "Tough night, huh?"

Uncle Isaac offers a response, "Pastor, some of us here took the life of another yesterday for the first time in that skirmish. Some people we knew died. It's difficult, right now."

The Pastor slows his walk, stops and responds attempting to rationalize. "Trouble with war is, both sides think their cause is right and noble."

"Yeah, well," Bobby setting his plate aside, continues his thoughts, "It's more than that. Like, what could happen in this here camp? One second we are standin' here lookin' 'round and the next second we are gone, gone I say, with an arrow through our heart. Aren't you scared? I mean, it could be a good guy like, Ben, or even you, pastor?"

"Yes, I'm a little nervous, but not about death. Cause I know where I'm going. I'm more queezy about how I'm going to die.

Yesterday was somewhat humbling. Maybe it's time to get yourselves right?"

Later in the afternoon as the coolness begins to settle in for the evening. Running Deer, walks through the smoldering ruins of his former home, takes a deep breath and sadly speaks to the warriors surveying the grounds with him and at the same time watching for Americans that might still be around.

"Even though I am pleased to know many braves from up north are organizing to come help us against the long-knives, Kekionga is no longer recognizable."

Merely two miles away in Chillicothe, E.J. eats a promised meal with Charlotte's family.

"How's your appetite, E.J.?" asks Charlotte. "This fish was caught today."

"The catfish is good, Charlotte, but my appetite is not that great. I'm still disturbed about yesterday."

"I can understand that."

"And, did you hear? We are heading back to Cincinnati, tomorrow mornin'. Maybe, a good night's rest will help. But I feel uneasy about leavin' here. It's like there's more to do."

Charlotte replies, "The army has already left its mark on the Miamitown villages."

"I know, but..."

Chapter 11

October 21, 1790 - Chillicothe

"The goal today...," says General Harmar to Lieutenant Ebenezer Denny hesitating. "What is this day, Denny, Thursday?"

"Yes sir, Thursday."

"The goal is to get to the same campsite we had on the 17th or the 16th, ah, I don't remember off hand. Have to check my diary. You know, you've done a good job keepin' us organized in camp. I like that map you made of Kekionga."

"Thank you, sir. It should illustrate to General St. Clair and Secretary Knox back in New York what it looks like out here."

Harmar continues the conversation. "We've lost a lot of packhorses on this journey, though. But, I think after catchin' red-handed those renegades two nights ago tryin' to steal our horses, our sentries are stayin' more alert."

"Maybe, sir," responds Denny climbing onto his saddled horse, "we're set to leave at your command. That campsite we want to get to will put us on the trail we came north on."

"Good, good," Harmar replies placing his foot into the stirrup of his mount. "Now scouts Williams and Dee know they're going to stay back and watch for an Indian build up at Kekionga, don't they?"

"Yes, sir. Major Whistler is in charge of that. Scouts'll let us know about any Injun activity. Are you ready to move out, sir? Shall we bring up the fife and drums?"

"What else can we do here, Lieutenant? We have destroyed, what did you say yesterday? 185 buildings of sorts and several thousand bushels of corn. Ransacked about everything they had. Other than the Eel River incident, it's been a good campaign."

"Well, catchin' the British and French traders was part of the plan, General," says Denny. "Those British Brown Bess muskets the redskins had up north in that skirmish were not good."

"I agree, Denny. I would have liked to have seen those scoundrels hangin' before we left. Perhaps we will see that happen another day. Yeah, what the heck? Let's go. Get 'em drummin' the assembly."

Returning Denny's salute, Harmar commands, "Get the colors up here. Let's march outta here with pride."

In Kekionga, the returned warriors stir around salvaging what they can and unburying items not found by the Americans. Nearby, Little Turtle holds a meeting with several chiefs.

"Here's the latest," Blue Jacket conveys. "In two days 700 Ottawa braves will be here from the big lakes region to help in an attack on the Americans. If the whites are leaving they cannot get that far away."

Nodding his head affirmatively, Little Turtle smiles at Blue Jacket and then looks at LeGris, "I agree. They have a long way to travel to the Ohio and we have plenty of ambush areas to choose from. Start thinking, LeGris, on that strategy."

"I'm getting quizzical looks," LeGris says standing up and looking around. "I don't mind helping with plans, but am I the only one that can sign around here, Turtle? Can't you see we have some new warrior chiefs sitting among us?"

"Yes, I can see that. Help us out though, LeGris, you're good at it," winking at Blue Jacket. "You know I get my tongue tied when I try to use sign language."

"Ah, Turtle," reacts Legris, "I never know when you are joking."

Spotting Running Deer foraging a former abundant garden, Little Turtle gives a whistle to him and waves him over. "We have a couple French speakers sitting over here," pointing to two chiefs. "Help them out, will you?"

"Of course," Running Deer responds in French and walking over to the chiefs.

"Our spies will watch the American movements," informs Little Turtle. "What do you say, Chief Richardville? We need a defense right here in Kekionga, in case the Americans come back."

"Ha. We have but 150 warriors against the American army of 1400, do I hear?" asks Richardville shaking his head. "You may want to leave again. There are no Miami villages to defend. Besides, most of our food for the winter has been destroyed. What do we eat?"

A Fox chief immediately jumps up and through an interpreter answers the last question. "The enemy and their horses are the food we can eat!"

Some stirring in agreement among the tribal leaders takes place.

Looking at the Chief of the Fox nation, Little Turtle speaks on. "We will rule nothing out." Then, turning toward and addressing Richardville, "This is still our home land. Maybe you did not suffer much damage in your villages farther up the St. Mary's River like we did, but our pride and self-confidence comes into decision making, occasionally."

"No disagreement there, Turtle," responds Richardville. "A strong message must be sent back with the long-knives to their president, Washington, if the Long-knives can make it."

Three miles south of Chillicothe, the now smaller American army, the results of desertions of militia and camp followers and casualties of battle, trudge in a southerly direction over uneven, sometimes marshy terrain.

"Doesn't it feel good to be headin' back to the Ohio River, E.J.?" asks Charlotte walking next to him and pulling a packhorse. "My family really likes you E.J. and I don't mind tellin' you I admire your courage at your age goin' on this mission. Father commented yesterday about you and your buddies helping stop that surge of Injuns comin' at ya down that trail."

"Gotta admit, Charlotte, I was scared, but something kicked in and we got it done. I like your family too, and well, I like... ah, gee we sure are missin' a lot of packhorses. This is gonna be a long march carryin' this stuff ourselves."

"It's alright, E.J.," enclosing his hand with hers, "we can make it."

In front of the military procession riding behind the cavalry and listening to drum and fife music heading south, are Harmar and his trusted officers.

"Perhaps to pick up the spirits of everyone we have a dance tonight?" suggests the General. "We have much to be thankful for and..."

"Pardon the interruption, sir," intervenes Major Whistler, "but in case you didn't notice we have people with us that cannot believe we aren't goin' back to Eel River and bury our dead. Some are ready to rebel against you, including some of the regulars."

"I can solve that, General," Colonel Hardin says eagerly joining the conversation. "Allow me to take a force back today. We will catch the Injuns by surprise and bury..."

"What's your take on this," interrupting and ignoring Hardin, "Major Ziegler?" asks Harmar.

"We have lost half our packhorses due to theft, neglect and starvation. The early frost ten days ago has taken away some foliage along the trail we were countin' on. The beeves we have remaining should get us back to the fort. A lot of muskets were lost in that panic, let's say, hasty retreat from the battle field. The general morale and lack of cooperation from the militia is the biggest issue, in my opinion, sir."

After a few moments of silent rumination while the drum and fife played on, Harmar breaks the silence, "I need to talk to the field officers tonight."

About 9 P.M. that evening in camp eight miles south of Kekionga, Harmar's meeting is stopped suddenly by the appearance of Chief Scout Daniel Williams.

"Well Danny, come in. We were all just talking about you and chatting about what may be happening out there. How 'bout a cup of rum?"

"Don't mind if I do. Thanks. Finding you was not that easy," says Williams

"Hope you know everybody."

The coonskin capped Williams nods about and then speaks. "General, I won't beat around the bush. The Injuns are back at Kekionga. A few at first that we kinda expected, but Johnny Dee and I figure a hundred, maybe more are settling in again."

"Let's get 'em General. Let's surprise 'em in the mornin'," Hardin encourages. "General," Hardin unremittingly talks as he stands up to pace around, "you and I both know that even General Washington wasn't the greatest strategist and that he lost far more battles than he won against the British during the Revolutionary War. But that crossing of the Delaware in the dead of winter at night to take Trenton, was daring and brilliant."

"I full well know what you are driving at, Colonel," says Harmar looking away, "but I have the responsibility to get these folks back safely whether they are a deadbeat substitute or a little girl of the camp followers."

"General, revenge and makin' up for the Eel River loss, would go a long way toward savin' face," offers Hardin hopefully convincingly.

"Two o'clock in the mornin' though. What are we doing?" asks Ben trudging toward the detachment General Harmar is ordering out. "We should be sleepin'."

"Let's see, there are three columns. We're over in the right column under our old friend from the Ohio River, Major McMillin," says

E.J. "But dang, they done split us up and put Bobby with Major Hall on the left."

"At least we got a full moon to light the way," offers Ben glancing up between the trees.

E.J., straining his eyes through the moonlit darkness spots his uncle. "Ike is up front with Fontaine again."

"I can't see even with a full moon," comments Ben. "I'm jus' gonna follow the guy in front of me."

"Wooo, that's me, Ben," says E.J turning around. "Careful. Keep your bayonet pointed up."

"Sorry, E.J."

"I can't believe no one from Pennsylvania, but us, wants to go. It sounds like a perfect plan to me. What do they know that we don't? Where's the bravery? I saw some guys cryin' back there."

"All I know is we are headin' back to Kekionga," counters Ben.

Chapter 12

October 22, 1790 - Kekionga

Traces of daylight from the clear mid-autumn dawn skies are beginning to take effect, when the 400 man American detachment led by Major John Wyllys pauses a half mile from the south river bank of the Maumee over-looking Kekionga.

"Dad burnit, I thought you knew your way around here, Williams," the frustrated Major Wyllys states after a planned three hour march stretches to four and a half. "The sun is coming up and we are losing the element of surprise if we don't get Hall, Ormsby, Hardin and their men around to the other side of the St. Joseph undetected."

"Sorry, Major. Things look different at night," apologizes the guide and scout.

"You know where to cross the St. Mary's at don't ya?" asks Wyllys.

"Yep, and I'm takin' 'em that way right now," Williams says, waving to Hall to bring his 150 man militia column up to follow him to the left.

Wyllys spots Hardin going by following Hall and whispers loudly, "Colonel, it's gotta be quick and it's gotta be quiet. Make sure none of your people fire a gun until you hear the sound of our attack, okay?"

"Yeah, I know the plan. But you betta' give us a good hour to get along that west bank before you commence," Hardin retorts harshly, still ticked he's not leading this offensive.

"Major Fontaine. Over here," orders Wyllys.

"Yes, Major. We are about ready to go," answers Fontaine in a low voice, pulling his horse up behind him by the reigns leaving his forty man cavalry back and unsaddled. "We are double checking the loading of the muskets and pistols as we speak."

"Well, don't be too anxious. In fact, keep the horses and the rattle of the sabers back here for a while. I'll send Private Smith in a little bit to let you know when to come forward. Grab some beef jerky or whatever."

At the same time the Americans are advancing for the attack and ambush, seventy five warriors are reclined catching their last bit of sleep around campfires in the desecrated Kekionga.

"Psst, Richardville," Little Turtle in a low voice speaks after rolling over toward him. "You sure our flanks are covered?"

Listing toward Little Turtle nearby, "Yes, warning spies are out there on both sides of us."

Little Turtle whispers back to him, "I can't help but feel a little uneasy. Harmar served with Washington against the British. I can't believe he is leaving us with that great big army of his."

"While you slept last night," Richardville responds, attempting to reassure, "I was told more Potawatomi and others have come in. They are aware of the defensive plan if we need it, and remain near the old British fort up the St. Joseph."

"Blue Jacket is still along the Maumee ford, correct?" asks Little Turtle.

"Yes. He has 50 warriors sleeping, hidden in the growth along the banks of our south buffer. Hopefully, this is all for nothing as we wait for the Ottawa warriors to join us tomorrow."

While the cavalry walk their horses past E.J. and Ben, and then bend east down the Maumee to its attacking point, Uncle Isaac leading his horse, slows by the boys and murmurs, "I'm proud of you guys, I'll see ya back at camp, if not sooner."

"Thanks, be careful, Unk," murmurs E.J.

"Good luck, Ike," responds Ben. "Glad we got to see Bobby, too," turning his attention to E.J. "Can't believe they wouldn't let him switch back to our company."

"Yeah, that Wyllys and Hall are real sticklers. Hardin would have allowed that. Probably a lot of requests goin' on. Gotta' draw the line somewhere."

Fifteen minutes later Major McMillin orders E.J.'s and Ben's column, "Stay low and move down to the right of the regulars. Stay back from the riverbank ten yards," commands Major McMillin. "Quiet and stay down."

As the 150 man militia company lines the south bank of the Maumee to the right of the sixty regulars, the cavalry stays back even farther than the infantry from the river, and guide their horses a quarter mile downriver. Scout Johnny Dee, leading Fontaine's cavalry, positions them at a lower bank leading to a shallow but deeper ford than Wyllys' men will have.

Almost a half mile west of what remains of the Kekionga village, Daniel Williams and Major Hall direct three companies of militia across the St. Marys River and march through forest toward Spy Run creek.

"Capturing and disposing of those native spies last night just may have saved our surprise, Hardin," Hall says following Williams and speaking quietly to the Colonel.

"It better have, because the information from 'em 'bout more Injuns comin' isn't comforting."

Hall looking back at the tailing companies, stops and utters, "Crap, get 'em up here, Colonel. They're laggin' and the suns almost up."

"I know. They been marchin' all night, Major" responds Hardin.

"Alright, alright. Here's where we're gonna split off. Okay, Danny?

"Yep, good as any place, I reckon," answers Williams.

"Now, as planned. I'm takin' my company through the forest a little while longer toward the old fort. Ormsby, take your column straight ahead through the cornfield to the river, but mind you, there won't be cover of darkness much longer and that field is charred. So stay low and be quick to the foliage along the bank. Hardin, same deal, stay low, be quick and take yours to the south edge of Frenchtown. Remember, let the Injuns come to you and pick'em off in the river."

A half hour later as Hall's column of militia nears where they want to depart from the forest an unsettling sound occurs.

Bam, bam, babam...

"That came from behind us on this side of the river," Bobby Conrad states to anyone in his column, commanded by Major Hall, that's listening. "We're not supposed to start the attack."

"Let's go," Hall says, "on the double, follow me." Leading his column on the run toward the bank of the river across from the former British fort, another shot is heard.

"One or two random shots is normal, maybe, but that was not," speaks Little Turtle jumping up to his feet to look around and assess the situation through the new morning daylight. "Brothers, take your positions."

Blue Jacket and his braves reclining among the north bank canes, weeds and trees of the Maumee, hear the shots also and the leader signals his warriors to stay hidden. Intentionally, he sends Running Deer and two other braves sprinting northeast along the river to see if there are any Americans on the south bank hidden and perhaps draw their fire. Major Wyllys and his troops, figuring correctly the surprise was ruined, ignore the decoys and advance down the steep bank and into the shallow crossing.

"Here they come," whispers Blue Jacket to William Wells while holding the palm of his out stretched hand down waiting for the Americans to reach mid-stream of the ford.

"Now, Blue Jacket, now!" Wells anxiously requests staring through the cover at the advancing invaders.

"Ahhhyyyya!" screams Blue Jacket raising his palm up.

Fifty staccato shots go off from the concealed Indians toward the surprised Americans. Then, because loading the muskets would take too long, the bow is used and arrows are projected through the smoke of the discharged guns.

Falling into the river around Wyllys are scattered regulars and three cavalrymen and their horses that were to assist Wyllys' charge into Kekionga.

"Dang, the Major didn't start this action but we're goin' now," says McMillin waving his arm to signal the militia under his command, to attack.

"Whoa," Ben yells as he missteps and tumbles down the bank rolling and losing a grip on his musket.

E.J., who safely slides down the decline, scoops up Ben's gun and hands it to him at the river's edge. "Come on, let's go."

As the two start into the river, musket fire from the Americans scatter the Indians on the opposite bank.

Crossing the river, high-stepping and then wading through deeper areas with the other 150 militia spread out semi straight lined, E.J. looks left and sees individual regulars and horses, a hundred yards away, laying and struggling in the shallow waters. "I think I saw Private Smith go down, Ben, dang."

"Look ahead, E.J.," replies Ben. "Those Injuns keep stoppin', popping up and firin' at us. Be ready to shoot when ya get a good shot!"

Militia, advancing in a wave, suffer scattered casualties out in the wide open river bed.

The two buddies noticing that, run in a stooped over fashion trying to make himself as small a target as he can. "McMillin's waving us to the right," says E.J.

The militia shifts to the right and rush through a garden observing the much faster cavalry unit way up ahead and farther to the right.

"Where's the cavalry goin'?" asks E.J.

"Dang. We're all gettin' separated, E.J.," Ben answers.

As the regulars and militia attempt to drive the Indians toward the St. Joseph River to the northwest and Major Hall's Americans, pockets of warriors jump up from behind burned village remains and fire their foreign made muskets.

Advancing, the militia return fire.

BAM.

"Good shot, E.J., stay here and reload. I'll cover ya," says Ben looking around. "Ought oh... the Injuns to our right, way over there, just pulled Fontaine off his horse and oh, crap. He's a goner. There's no help over there! How'd the cavalry get all spread out? Ike's gotta be over... oh, they gotta 'nother one of ours."

"Okay, I'm ready. Let's move to the left toward the St. Joe at least," suggests E.J. "I can't see very well... too much smoke. Yeah, I think that's McMillin wavin' at us to move that way anyway."

The Indian strategy of spreading the Americans out lead to isolated bayonet and tomahawk battles taking place with fatal consequences. A few Indians lure the whites forward toward more damaged Kekionga huts and cabins where Miami and other braves wait in ambush.

"Man, you're fast! Good job!" barks Little Turtle to Running Deer passing him by with a perfect dive roll into cover. "Load up! Here we go!" orders the Miami Chief, "AHHHYAA!"

Fifty warriors jump up and ignite their muskets at the ensuing Americans and this time both regulars and militia, focusing on this area of Kekionga, go down. Those not hit return fire and doggedly pursue into the smoky Indian cover for more fierce combat.

"Hey, look at me!" yells a warrior in Algonquin while putting Wyllys' fancy officer's hat on and slicing through the injured Major's top head with a scalping knife. "AHHHYAA!"

"I'll ahhhhyaa you!" a regular, nearby speaking under his breath reacts by ramming his bayonet through the pompous brave.

On the west side of the St. Joseph River watching much of the Kekionga battle, is Colonel Hardin's portion of Major Hall's militia force.

"We gotta get over there, Colonel!" urges a Kentuckian.

"We gotta follow orders and wait for the redskins to cross the river toward us for the ambush, dang it! It does look kinda bad, but the smoke and haze is obscuring much of it."

"Guys I know are over there, Colonel," insists another militiaman.

Colonel Hardin surveils out loud, "the fightin's all movin' north along the river! Hey, up the river Injuns crossing but no one's firin' at 'em! That's Ormsby's area. Must be a gap between us. Let's go, we're gonna move our column that way. Follow me!" Hardin commands.

The militia, under Major McMillin's leadership in Kekionga, start bending their efforts east to west toward the Miamitown fighting near the St. Joseph River.

ZING!

"Dang. Where'd that shot come from?" says Ben. "That Kentuckian to my left just went down. I gotta help."

"No, we gotta keep goin', Ben, or we'll be next. See how the Injuns are doin' it? Hit and then run. Keepin' on the move," recommends E.J.

"Yeah, I see how. We'll help that guy later."

"Have your pistol ready, Ben," warns E.J. "We're headin' into some..."

Sporadic shooting is everywhere with gunpowder smoke filling the air. Hand to hand fighting between whites and Native Americans take place mainly because there is no time to reload and both sides take advantage of an enemy combatant trying to do that with a bayonet stab.

"Stay together, Ben," urges E.J.

Bam!

"Dang! How did I miss that young redskin?" complains Ben. "Look at him go!

Bam! "Dang it! That return shot just nicked my ear, E.J.!"

"Let's go, Ben. Bayonet charge. They're running on up the river toward that old fort."

"Hold up, E.J.," says his buddy pointing to his right. "McMillin's signaling again. He wants everybody over by him."

"Maybe it's over," replies E.J. "We're lettin''em run off."

"Maybe, but, look around, we've lost a bunch of guys."

Little Turtle leads the Indian withdraw from Miamitown toward the Potawatomi force waiting up the St. Joseph River in thickets on top of higher ground. A few frightened Indians begin to run across the river toward the northwest trail to escape the chaos and are met with musket fire from Major Hall's militia contingent on the west bank.

"Follow the plan!" yells Little Turtle waving the warriors back up the east bank.

"I think we can hit some of them from here," exclaims Bobby Fulton reloading and then taking aim with his fellow infantry.

"Yeah, see what you can do!" orders Hall.

The shots from the militia across the river drive the Indians back inland out of range.

"Hey, you three over there," Hall directs pointing to his right. "Yeah, you three. Watch our backside. I've seen some problems down river. Injuns been attackin' from behind."

Major McMillin brings his troops together. "Hey, dad burn it, we are not fallin' for another ambush. Be smart."

"Major, take a look at...", E.J. says pointing across a flattened cornfield.

The cavalry with thirty riders gallop toward the conflict after being diverted further east chasing Indians. Now refocused with sabers drawn they are joining the battle.

"That's Uncle Ike up front, Ben, on that grey mare leadin' the charge."

Spreading out with muskets reloaded, the foot soldiers try to time the attack with the cavalry. Brandishing their already stained bayonets they head toward the concealed Indians on the higher ground.

Seven of Hall's Kentuckians west of the St. Joseph River cannot contain themselves, disobey orders, and charge down the bank and cross the river heading toward the old dilapidated fort area.

Once again the American advance is met with musket fire from the hidden warriors and then meeting the surviving attackers with deadly hand weapons.

"Ben!" screams E.J. on his back about to receive a tomahawk to the chest.

Glimpsing this, Ben draws out his flintlock pistol shooting the brave before he could deliver the blow.

Rolling away, E.J. looks up to see Ben winking at him and then witnessing the side of Ben's head being bashed by an Indian's war club.

Infuriated, E.J. grabs his musket, leaps to his feet and singles out the offending warrior, chasing him down, and ending his life with his bayonet.

Looking east into the smoke and haze across the river, six of Hall's men are thinking they are seeing Indians mounted on horses. With intentions to help their fellow Americans, they fire blindly into the intense fighting.

"Cease fire, you fools! Our men are in that. That's our cavalry," Major Hall states with exasperation.

"Retreat across the river! Get across the river!" orders Major McMillin repeatedly amongst the chaos. "Draw them to the ambush!"

Regulars, militia and cavalry try to disengage from the fighting and head for the St. Joseph River bank, but the relentless warriors follow in pursuit dragging soldiers down from behind.

Tumbling down the fifteen foot sloped embankment of the river and losing his Charleville is E.J. with Running Deer closing in on him carrying a tomahawk. Musketless, E.J. scrambles to his feet and runs. Slipping on the wet river rock underfoot, E.J. falls again and is at the mercy of the swift approaching Miami warrior.

Sighting E.J.'s dilemma, Bobby charges down to the river's edge, raising and aiming his rifle at Running Deer, and then shoots. Through the black powder smoke he sees the young brave, three feet from E.J., dropping his tomahawk and grabbing his wrist.

Several hollering militia charge by Bobby joining the melee taking place on the mid-river rocks.

Running Deer fends off Americans effectively with one hand as a skirmish takes place between cavalry, regulars, militia and the redskin coalition. Combatants from both sides are either fleeing the melee or entering the confusing fracas.

The remaining forces with Hall, atop the west bank, are joined by Colonel Hardin's and Ormsby's companies of eighty Kentuckians approaching along the top of the bank single file from the south.

Not knowing how many Americans are following Hardin and Ormsby's units, Little Turtle calls for a retreat.

The braves scatter up and down the river and ascend the banks. Some run across to scramble up the west bank.

With shots sounding occasionally from the Americans to finish off injured Indians and wounded horses struggling to get up from the riverbed, Hall warns the just arriving Hardin. "Them varmints been attacking us on the backside, too, here. See them crossin' up there? This fightin' may not be over."

"Yeah, I see it," says Hardin. "Let's gather the injured and make our way back to Harmar's camp. Where's Major Wyllys?"

Shaking his head, "Haven't seen him," answers Major Hall, taking command. "Come on men, let's go! Get up here before the Injuns reorganize! Fulton, yeah, you, Bobby! You and your buddy, there. Pick up another gun if you don't have one. There's plenty to pick from. Load it. What are you waitin' on? Watch our backside as we get outta the river bed."

"Yes, sir," answers Bobby.

"Where's Uncle Ike?" asks a dazed E.J. looking around, "where's my Uncle Isaac? I don't... don't see him. I gotta go back up there and find him," he murmurs, beginning to walk easterly.

Grabbing his friend by the shoulder, Bobby redirects him. "Come on E.J., we gotta follow orders. Where's Ben?" asks Bobby.

Chapter 13

October 22-23, 1790 - Kekionga

At the Maumee River ford, in the late afternoon, where some of Major Wyllys' troops and horses were the first casualties of the day that morning, war whoops of celebration take place mid-stream. Indians dance while stripping off usable clothing and taking weapons from the dead American bodies. Scalping and mutilation occurs to gain reward from the British and chase the spirits of the whites away.

Indians wave scalps above their heads and celebrate in their minds another great victory over the enemy.

"Holy Moses," murmurs Private John Smith to himself lying injured along the river's south edge among the debris of logs and branches, watching. With a musket ball lodged in his thigh he waits for nightfall to make his slow retreat undetected.

"The Ottawa will join us tonight," informs the blood stained legged Blue Jacket to Little Turtle and LeGris on shore viewing the gleeful warriors. "Then we can finish off the Americans tomorrow."

"Yes," Little Turtle acknowledges, "let's finish off the invaders before they get any further away. This time the numbers will favor us. What you say, LeGris?"

"Our spies have observed the defeated Americans retreating to Harmar's camp a few miles from here. They appear stunned. The long knife leader still has surrounded himself with many regulars, though."

"Yes," Blue Jacket asserts, "but with the 700 Ottawa and others coming in, victory over them tomorrow is assured. Then, no white will ever want to come back to our homes."

"Nothing is for sure, Blue Jacket," professes LeGris, "but I tend to agree. Our strategy will be to surround and slowly squeeze. No escape. Finish them all off," concludes a grimacing LeGris.

At the American camp, mid-afternoon, eight miles south of Kekionga, anxiousness pervades the atmosphere.

"Scout's comin' in, sir!" yells a sentry guard.

General Harmar sitting on a log near his campfire, springs to his feet spilling his mug of hot cider. "Well, bring him in. Get him some water to drink or somethin'!" orders Harmar

"Johnny Dee reporting, sir."

"Yeah, I know who you are. What happened back there?"

"Major Hall and Hardin drove the Injuns from the battlefield, sir, but we suff..."

"That's great. Did you hear that, Major Whistler? I knew that early mornin' ambush would work. Get over here, Lieutenant Denny. Were you doubting this? Ah, I never know with you. How far away is Wyllys' detachment, Dee?"

"A couple miles, comin' up the trail yet."

"Whistler," requests the General, "send a company out there to meet them. They should receive a grand return greeting."

"Gener'al," Dee hesitating to burst Harmar's elation. "It was a very deadly battle."

Nightfall in Kekionga has campfires with stew boiling in kettles brought in from Chief Richardville's camp to replace the ones taken during the American pillage. The population has swollen with more local returning braves, and a huge influx of Ottawa, Fox and Wea warriors from the north after they heard of the victories over the Americans.

"The chiefs of these new warriors are glad the braves that have died have been taken care of," interprets Chief LeGris sitting by the main fire to all that surrounds it. "They are curious, though, on where the tastiness of the stew comes from. They notice the devastation of Kekionga's gardens and fields as well as the houses and still dead strewn horses and bodies of the Americans."

"Tell them, LeGris, much of their courage tomorrow morning will come from the fallen Americans," declares a Miami sub chief stirring the kettle in charge of food.

"The full moon," observes Blue Jacket, "will guide us to our attacking points before sunrise tomorrow morning. Running Deer, you fought bravely today. Will your hand be ready for the morning?"

"The desire to drive the Americans from our land, chief Blue Jacket, outweighs any injury. My Manitou strengthens and sustains me. The shaman around here work the Kitchi Manitou powers to heal whatever injuries our proud warriors have."

In Harmar's camp the attitude is different.

"We demand that we go back and bury our loved ones!" yells a near hysterical widow above the din of other camp followers assembled outside of Harmar's tent.

"Keep them back," orders Lieutenant Denny to his regulars assigned to guard the General.

Inside the tent, discussions take place on what to do next.

"I count 150 minimum lost today, General," updates an exhausted Major McMillin. Fifty of sixty regulars gone, sir. Fine soldiers. Fought with honor. The Kentuckians for the most part did too. Made up for Eel River. A hundred of them did not come back with us and are assumed dead. It was most assuredly a brave effort."

"Don't like losing Wyllys, Fontaine... any of them," states General Harmar, no longer elated. "But I still consider it a victory. How many Indians did we kill?"

"Optimistically," answers McMillin, "maybe as many as we lost."

"I need a full report of today's action in forty eight hours. This campaign has been a huge success with five villages pillaged and destroyed. Much of their winter food destroyed. Many of the natives killed."

"That part has been good, sir," Whistler says.

"Alright, listen up," Harmar begins clearing his throat and lowering his voice. "Keep this under your hat. This is not over yet. Danny Williams says there are many Indians coming into Kekionga from the north."

"Major Hall and I can confirm that, General," inserts Colonel Hardin. "The captured Spy we questioned this morning said the same."

"Gentlemen," continues Harmar, "we cannot go back there at this time. It would be farcical to call this an army to be reckoned with. We gotta move south in the morning."

"General," Whistler chimes in again, "half the camp will applaud that decision. Many want to leave right now."

Harmar urgently adds, "We can't cause a panic. All of you here, advise your officers to spread the word we are still waiting on stragglers. Any disobedience by anybody will be met harshly. Tell them to be on high alert. We'll head to Fort Washington at ahh, yeah, let's move it up from our normal time to 9 A.M."

Later that night, E.J. and others around campfires try to comprehend what happened that day.

"Surely we will go back in the mornin' to find Uncle Isaac and Ben, or they will come walkin' into camp any minute now, don't ya think?" asks E.J.

Charlotte, attempting to comfort E.J. interjects. "As we have heard, men in the battle witnessed them bein', well, ya know... I'm sorry, E.J."

"Pastor," inquires E.J. looking for answers, "do you think Uncle Isaac and Ben got themselves right with God before today?"

Bobby shaking his head, still trying to grasp the day's battle, intercepts the question. "E.J. that might be the last thing the Pastor would know."

"Actually, I did talk to your Uncle Isaac awhile back, E.J. We had a long talk. He told me how much he loved and misses his wife and family. But, he considers you guys his family, now. The bodies may be lifeless but their souls are with God," consoles the Pastor. "I spoke to both of them privately more recently. They're okay, but how 'bout you folks?"

"Here E.J., Bobby, have a little more cider," offers Charlotte. "What are you talkin' about, Pastor? The awful Indians took them from us."

"Whoa, take a look at the eclipse, tonight!" Pastor says with amazement, pointing up with his right hand. "We are in for a show." Lowering his arm and shaking his head slowly he asks, "Tell me these heavenly spectacles are just an accident? The earth's shadow fits perfectly over the moon. You folks ever seen a solar eclipse?"

"I don't think so," murmurs Bobby slightly interested.

"Moon fits perfectly in front of the sun during that eclipse. Well, ah, I need to move on to another family and see some more people. I'll be around if you need me."

Back in Kekionga, Little Turtle is awakened by Blue Jacket just as the total lunar eclipse is halfway through.

"They're leaving!" declares Blue Jacket shaking Little Turtle. "Tomorrow's victory is not happening."

"What? What's going on?" asks Little Turtle. "What is all the commotion? Who is leaving, Blue Jacket?"

"The Shaman indicate it is a sign from Kitchi Manitou. The Manitou are insistent. Look," says Blue Jacket, pointing up to the star splashed night sky and the rare sight of the eclipse.

"That is definitely a sign," concedes Little Turtle.

"The Ottawa unquestionably take this as a forewarning of a devastating defeat from the whites if we strike them," utters Blue Jacket. "They are leaving now. So are other tribal warriors. They are going home."

CHAPTER 14

Spring, 1912 - Lakeside Park Area, Fort Wayne, Indiana

"Now you boys are sayin' all you was doing was digging a foundation footer for this here house?" asks the Allen County Sheriff.

"Yes, sir," responds Nyle.

"We didn't do anything, Sheriff, honest," expresses Stan. "Tell 'em, Mr. Gavin."

"Let's see your building permits, boys," demands the Sheriff. "Cordon off the area, deputies. Keep the onlookers back. There ain't that much to see, anyway, yet."

"Come on Reichelderfer, quit scaring these guys," complains Bob Gavin. "You know there have been plenty of old remnants found in these parts. Just bring in Klaehn's to help remove these bones as the men put in the foundation. The undertakers, for Pete's sake, can rebury 'em at Lindenwood or Concordia."

"Ha. Had ya goin' didn't I boys?" smiles the Sheriff.

"Whew, yeah a little bit," proclaims Stan.

"Forgive me, okay?" replies the Sheriff. "I get bored dealin' with drunks and their issues all the time. This stuff is kinda gruesome but yet interesting, isn't it?"

"Didn't you guys deal with finding an old musket down that St. Joseph riverbank, over there, a few years back?" asks Bob Gavin.

"Yes siree, Bob. Sheriff Clausmeier back in 1894, if I remember right, investigated an old French Charleville found in the sand at water's edge. Had a bayonet, too. It's in some museum somewhere out east, last I heard. Some other musket parts and bent up bayonets were discovered some time back over in the Maumee on the other side of Lakeside. Musta been some kinda battle here."

Later that night the funeral service employees remove exposed bones and skulls from the housing site that were uncovered during the day by the construction workers.

"Jake, for some reason I feel a bit uncomfortable picking up these bones tonight."

"Well, I don't know why. We've done other cemetery removals after dark before. Move that lantern over a little bit, will ya, Josh? Okay. There, that's better."

"Yeah. The curious sure like to see this type a thing, it seems. Hard to get much done with folks gettin' in the way during the day."

"Ok, I'd say we need to take this stretcher full over to the hearse," suggests Jake. "We got quite a bit on here."

"Yep. Hey, place the lantern on the stretcher too. Ready? Up we go. Watch your step, Jake."

"Horses seem a bit jumpy. You got the brake on the wagon don't ya?"

"Think so."

"*That you, Ben?*"

"*Uncle Ike?*"

"You say somethin', Josh?"

"Uh... ah... I was gonna ask you the same thing."

Accreditation and Further Reading

The Pictorial History of Fort Wayne - *B.J. Griswald*

General Josiah Harmar's Campaign Reconsidered: How the Americans Lost the Battle of Kekionga - *Michael S. Warner*

Miami Indians Facts, Information, Pictures - www.encyclopedia.com

The Military Journal of Major Ebenezer Denny, an Officer in the Revolutionary and Indian War - *Ebenezer Denny*

www.ohiohistorycentral.org

Flatboats on the Ohio River - *Deborah Heal*

www.patriotshistoryusa.com - Mike Fink, King of the River - *Mike Allen, Western Rivermen*

President Washington's Indian War, The Struggle for the Old Northwest - *Wiley Sword*

A Map of the Historic Maumee River - *Robert Ernst*

Re-evaluating "The Fort Wayne Manuscript": William Wells and the Manners and Customs of the Miami Nation - *William Heath*

Map of Indiana, the Influence of the Indian upon its History with Indian and French names for Natural and Cultural Locations - *E.Y. Guernsey, Indiana Department of Conservation, 1933. Stored in the Lincoln Collection, Lincoln Library, Allen County Public Library, Fort Wayne, IN.*

www.libraryofcongress.gov - The Proceedings of a Court of Inquiry held at the Special Request of Brigadier General Josiah Harmar to Investigate His Conduct as Commanding Officer of the Expedition Against the Miami Indians, 1790.

www.indianahistory.org - Chapter 1, Indiana Historical Society.

On the Trail of the Nephilim - *L.A. Marzulli*

The Holy Bible - *Genesis 6:4; Ecclesiastes 3:1-8; the Old and New Testament*

www.bonesofkekionga.com